MAGNOLIA LANE

Donald R. Guillory

This book is dedicated to the endless search for the truth. The words on the pages contained in this book could not be accomplished without the support of my family and the untold number of ghosts that haunted me as I punched letters on my keyboard making them come back to life.

Also, special thanks to The Spice Girls, Sam Cooke, Nina Simone, Bacardi, Havana Club Rum, *carne asada*, and, of course, reruns of "The Office."

1

Victoria prided herself in the woman she had become.

Standing on her balcony, she looked off to the horizon thinking of all the trauma, violence, and bloodshed she had witnessed on her two–thousand–acre empire. Her husband, Charles, long dead, had left her a struggling plantation with under one hundred slaves to tend the fields. Upon his death, a curse had been lifted from the grounds. Within two years under her authority, the land transformed from five hundred acres of struggling farmland to one of the most productive and profitable sugar and rice plantations in the south.

Taking in a deep breath of the night air,

Victoria continued writing in her leather–bound book. Stuffed with letters, documents, and her personal reflections, the book held the history of the Magnolia. The peace she found in her moment of contemplation was disturbed as she looked to the horizon seeing the dancing of lights breaking through the darkness of the night as they approached her home. Her gaze met the bearers of the torches encroaching on her land.

"What is it now?" she muttered.

She stared at the men as they drew closer. Victoria did not move from her position on the balcony.

"Miss Vickie!" one of the men shouted at her.

"Madame Blanc," she corrected him.

"We've tried to tolerate you. But you've pushed our patience to the limit."

"Do tell," she retorted as she lit a cigar.

"You see, we don't mind you keeping to yourself. In fact, we prefer it that way. We don't have an issue with you running your land the way that you do... but we can't have you riling up the nigras in town with talk of voting."

She was unmoved.

The man cleared his throat. "You see... um... well... there is a certain order that must be maintained."

"What 'order' is that?" she asked, tapping

the ash from the end of her cigar.

"Ma'am. We have been pushed too far and we won't tolerate losing more of what we have."

Victoria took another puff from her cigar.

"Ma'am. The black folks was just fine in this town before the war. They are still fine. Why do they need to risk losing everything they have by voting? They don't know how to run government. They cain't read or write. God put them on this Earth to be the wretches that they are... no more... no less. Why ridicule God by questioning what he made and try to undo it?"

"How am I undoing it?" she scoffed.

"Ma'am, by getting them to vote. Won't no good come of it."

"And why is that?"

"Ma'am, they are not equipped to lead themselves, much less, white men. If we let them get the vote, they could lord over all of us, including you!" he said, his face growing redder.

"You are mistaken, no one lords over me... never have, never will," she responded. "And I am not one to be intimidated by the likes of you or any other white men here. Now, if you please, you and the rest of your trash, get off my land," she followed, laying her shotgun on the balcony railing.

The men below stared up to her, not knowing what their next step would be. Assuming their show of numbers would be enough to dissuade her, the men huddled together, devising their next course of action.

Watching from her perch, Victoria aimed her shotgun at the ground below. Without warning, Victoria pulled the trigger, firing near her unwelcome guests. Startling the men and their horses, several fled from the building. The stalwarts of the group rushed forward. Victoria, alone in the house, grabbed her book and shotgun from the balcony, entering her bedroom.

Kneeling on the ground, she flipped over the rug before pulling up one of the floorboards. With the plank dislodged, she pulled out a small wooden chest. Fearing the men's intentions, she placed her book into the coffer before returning the floorboard. Beads of sweat ran down her brow as She heard the commotion of the men downstairs. Flipping the rug back over, Victoria waited for the men to enter her bedroom.

The trespassers charged forward to the building. Breaking through the French doors of the entrance, they stomped up the stairs leading to the bedroom Victoria occupied.

As the first man passed through the threshold of the room, his chest was ripped open by a blast of buckshot. Jeffrey's body fell to the floor as blood pour from his torso. Victoria stood at the far end of the room, aiming her shotgun in their direction as smoke billowed from the barrel. The intruders paused as a large crimson pool formed at their feet.

Victoria's eyes narrowed as she took aim at the raiding party. She pulled the trigger again. The impact decapitated one of the aggressors, spreading his blood and grey matter onto the door frame. Victoria smiled as she saw the remaining three men look on in horror.

Laurence DuPont, the leader of this motley crew ran toward Victoria as she reloaded. She met his advance, lowering her shoulder into his sternum. Momentarily shaken, Laurence grabbed the barrel, still warm from its firing, as he attempted to wrestle it out of Victoria's hands.

"Shoot her, goddammit!" Laurence yelled at his friends.

"You're in the way!" they responded, frustrated.

Feeling her hold of the weapon weaken, Victoria threw her right hand forward, raking Laurence's eyes. He roared in agony as he released his grip on the shotgun. His body shuffled between Victoria and his comrades. They could not fire upon her without injuring their friend. Reloading the shotgun, Victoria aimed it at the three men occupying her room. Pulling both triggers, she dispensed the full contents of the the two barrels at her foes.

The shot cut through the left side of Christopher's face, dislodging his ear. Mark and Richard were not as lucky. The shot reached Richard, impacting his eyes. The searing pain forced him to drop his rifle. The butt, striking the floor, forced the weapon to fire. The bullet sailed through the bottom of Mark's jaw and exited through the top of his skull, killing him instantly.

Laurence charged forward, launching himself into Victoria. His momentum pushed Victoria over the balcony railing. Her hands, moist from her sweat, the humidity, and her attackers' blood, failed to secure a grip on the wooden frame.

Slipping, her hands released from the railing. Falling from the balcony, Victoria spun in the air. Hitting the ground, feet first, her body slumped backward. Landing on her back, her neck whipped toward the ground; the back of her head impacting the ground, she was disoriented. Her ears rang. Turning on her stomach, Victoria attempted to stand. She drove her right foot into the ground. Denied by a sharp pain in her leg, she fell back to the ground.

Victoria was bloody, bruised, and broken. Wiping the blood from her mouth, she saw the face of Francis LeMonde looking down on her as she knelt. Grimacing, she spat blood onto the earth.

"We tried to warn you, but you wouldn't listen," he said kneeling over her, offering a handkerchief. "My patience has run its course."

Before Victoria could offer a reply or witty retort, she felt the presence of a rope around her neck. It tightened, restricting her ability to breathe. She heard Christopher's voice from the balcony calling for the rope to be thrown to him. He quickly slung it over the balcony, dropping the other end to the ground.

One end of the rope was connected to the noose around her neck while the other was in the hands of Francis. He dropped his end and grasped the noose around Victoria's neck. He pulled the rope tighter. Francis took the other end in hand. Victoria felt the pull of the rope. She struggled to give herself some comfort or possible release from the grip it had formed. Francis tugged and pulled, tightening the noose around Victoria's neck. The other men of the party pulled their end of the rope from above. With each tug, Victoria felt her body being dragged like a marionette. She fought against the force that was drawing her backward. Francis continued to pull on the noose as Victoria's feet ceased touching the ground. Tying the rope to one of the pillars at the entrance, the men watched as Victoria's legs dangled in the air as she fought off death.

Francis calmly walked over to Victoria. Her eyes were wide open. Her mouth was agape. He stood in front of Victoria, listening to her gurgle and choke on her blood and saliva.

"We warned you," he repeated. "Look at you now."

"Francis," she said, gasping. He stepped closer to listen to her. He lowered his face to hers. "Francis," she said with a gurgle.

"Yes?"

"Go to hell," she said before spitting in his face.

He chuckled for a slight moment with her blood and saliva on his face. Francis moved behind Victoria, grabbing the rope with one hand and placed his other on the top of the knot.

"After you," he whispered in her ear. Francis pulled on the rope forcefully, tightening the noose even more around Victoria's neck. She struggled, kicked, and clawed, but it was all in vain. Francis held the rope until he felt no life in her body.

Victoria's body lightly swung from side to side as Christopher and Francis carried their friends out of the building. They loaded the men on their horses and quietly rode off the property, content in their actions.

Dripping from her body, Victoria's blood formed a small pool on the ground below. Her body went cold.

2

Present

The sign reading "MAGNOLIA TOURS" swayed as a gentle breeze brushed against it. The sign squeaked lowly as it swung from the overhang. Sitting behind his podium, Terrance awaited the opportunity to answer any questions about the tour and book any of those passersby who were interested in taking the tour.

Terrance's job had become quite simple after the owner decided to make online reservations available. Despite this, he still wanted someone to man the booth in the likelihood of a visitor to the city wanting to take a tour of the "Crescent City" before the mystique had worn off.

Robert pulled the tour bus to the curb.

The squeal of the brakes disturbed Terrance's daydreaming as the vehicle approached. Years of working at the stand had made many of Terrance's actions become second nature. He walked up to the door and changed the tour sign on the bus from "The Majesty of The Magnolia" to one that read "The Magnolia in the Moonlight."

Robert stepped down from the converted streetcar sucking his teeth as he pulled out a pack of cigarettes from his breast pocket. He tapped the packet roughly before pulling out a single cigarette and popping it into his mouth. As it dangled from his bottom lip, he smiled at Terrance.

"Hey, T," he said in a friendly tone.

"Welcome back, Bobby," Terrance replied.

Stretching his arms out wide and cracking his neck, Robert asked, "So, how many do we have for 'Moonlight' tour?"

"Roughly a dozen. From the looks of this, it should be a lively group."

"Why's that?" Robert asked.

"Well, seven of them booked together and in the notes section they entered 'first time in New Orleans.' Celebrating our joint bachelor/ bachelorette party."

"Holy shit, that is stupid," Robert laughed, nearly swallowing his cigarette. "All the bars, strip clubs, and activities to be had in this city and they want to check out the city sites, a cemetery, and an old plantation in preparation for their nuptials? I really want to dislike tourists, but they make our jobs so enjoyable sometimes."

Robert looked at his watch. Seeing as he had several hours before the next tour, he walked inside of the building, signaling to Terrance that he would be taking his customary afternoon nap in order to be well-rested for the evening tour. Terrance, having completed the change of the signage on the bus, ran through his cleaning and inspection of it. After completing the review, he locked the bus up and sat back down at the booth awaiting any possible foot traffic.

3

The sun hung lazily on the horizon. Terrance looked at his watch and pushed a button on the booth that was connected to a buzzer upstairs awakening Robert. As the guests arrived, Terrance stamped their hands for entry onto the bus. Robert emerged from the building with a bright grin and his sharp wit. He greeted the patrons on the bus, giving them a short introduction of himself and a history of the converted streetcar that now served as their tour bus while they waited for all who would be taking the tour.

Robert recited the script, making it his own personal pitch from the first day he worked for the tour company. He memorized the tour information after practicing in front of a mirror for hours before he went in for his interview. Twenty years later, he could give the full tour blindfolded and hogtied, as he would often brag to tourists. He jokingly stated, on occasion, that in all of his years of doing the tours no one took him on the challenge.

As the passengers all settled into their seats, Robert advised them of the rules of the tour.

"It's pretty simple," he stated. "No smoking on the bus and please feel free to ask any questions at any time. You are more likely to forget what you may want to ask me than I am to forget what it is that I will talk about on the tour. Please feel free to eat and drink on the bus, but please make sure to make use of all trash receptacles provided. Also, be sure to laugh at all my jokes, or I will murder you and leave your body in the swamps. If you enjoy the tour or if you want to be sure that I don't murder you, please leave a nice tip in the gratuity box at the completion of the tour."

There were several chuckles from the crowd as Robert took his seat behind the steering wheel.

"That isn't funny," a young woman near the back of the bus whispered to her fiancé.

"Lois, calm down. It's just a joke. I mean, we are going on a tour of cemeteries and a plantation. Having a dark sense of humor is to be expected."

Her face soured as he did not express his support for her outrage at Robert's choice of humor.

"Brian," she said, grabbing his arm.

"Look, I'm not going to ruin this tour over a joke," Brian responded.

Marcus, sitting behind them, stretched his arm out, snapping his wrist to mimic a whipping motion. Brian, turning his head, looked directly at his friend, mouthing the words, *"fuck you"* before facing forward again in his seat.

Across the aisle sat Brian's sister, Lucinda. She accompanied her brother on the trip seeking the opportunity to finally convince Brian that he should not go through with marrying Lois. She never liked her. Lucinda saw Lois as someone who saw Brian as nothing more than a fad or phase. She once overheard Lois joke with her friends that she would marry someone like Brian just to get back at her parents. Lucinda was immune to Lois' charm, despite her attempts to win her over. Lucinda detested how Brian's Alabama sweetheart referred to herself as a "dainty Southern Belle."

Lucinda sighed and thought about what she could say that would have some meaningful impact on her brother. She didn't like the fact that Marcus had been little help on the trip other than his needling of Brian. They were like brothers and had known each other since their days of playing junior varsity baseball. He was not always the greatest influence on Brian, but his perspective was always welcome and appreciated. Unfortunately, on this matter, Marcus was hesitant to give Brian the push that he desperately needed.

Near the middle of the bus sat Calista. Her nose was buried in a book about Marie Laveau, *Voodoo Queen of New Orleans*. She sat quietly, with her knees to her chest, reading about the life and legends surrounding one of the city's most famous residents. Calista decided to take the tour as part of her love of the dark history of American cities.

She had only visited New Orleans once before, but as it was a family trip and she was only twelve at the time, she did not have the opportunity to enjoy New Orleans the way that she would have wanted. To her, there was nothing enjoyable about visiting riverboats and museums. Calista was much more enthralled with the idea of visiting places where history had taken place. Seeing artifacts or perfectly manicured displays did little to satisfy her curiosity.

She lifted her eyes above the pages to scan her surroundings, trying as best she could to profile those on the trip so she could play her own little game in her head to see if she was accurate at pegging personalities and backgrounds.

Seated across from Calista was a group of co–workers who were in town for a convention. They had all been looking forward to pursuing the offer when it was first announced in a company–wide email.

Although Panopticorps saw this as an opportunity for their employees to gain contacts and better develop their sales and management skills, Eli, Trudy, Anne, Margaret, and Eric all saw this as a chance for their employer to send them to New Orleans, all expenses paid. Rather than attend panels, listen to speakers, or participate in workshops, the six of them focused on food, drink, and relaxation.

As Robert finished his last few checks, three young women knocked on the door's window. Daphne, Dolores, and Donna stood outside the streetcar with the stamps on their hands.

Robert opened the door for the last–minute arrivals and quickly crossed them off the manifest. The three women bounced down the aisle approaching their seats in front of Brian, Lois, and Lucinda.

"Dun, Dun, Dun," Marcus said, laughing from his seat. "We almost made it."

"What took you so long?" Lois asked, gritting her teeth.

"Yeah. And why couldn't you take longer?" Marcus joked.

Lois turned to Marcus, shooting him a glance indicating that she had grown tired of his flippant attitude and remarks.
Avoiding her fury, Marcus buried himself in his phone, reviewing the profiles of the single women he found on his dating app. Lois returned her focus to her friends.

"Why are you just getting here?"

Daphne lowered her sunglasses, leaning into the seat in front of Lois.

"We decided to do some more day drinking. Just because you want to come to one of the funnest cities in the world and have the least amount of fun doesn't mean that we have to."

Lois fumed.

Donna and Dolores dropped themselves in a seat while Daphne found her resting spot across from them.

Lois gritted her teeth and muttered, "I have to be a babysitter on my own bachelorette week."

Robert turned the ignition initiating a smooth rumble throughout the bus.

Marcus patted the back of Brian and Lois' seat indicating his enthusiasm, annoying his friend's fiancé.

4

The bus exited the French Quarter on North Rampart Street and headed to the St. Louis Cemetery. Robert used the PA system to inform his riders on the history of the city as they came to each landmark. With each site they passed, Robert had a joke or anecdote to keep his passengers informed, engaged, and entertained. During the one stop before the Magnolia, he descended the bus telling them about some of the lore, legends, and myths regarding the individuals currently residing in St. Louis Cemetery.

After their time viewing the graves and crypts on the grounds, Robert and those on the tour returned to the bus for their final destination: The Magnolia.

During the thirty–minute voyage, Robert continued to entertain his passengers giving them bits of history mixed with a little fiction and fantasy to keep their interest. The passengers engaged in conversation as they watched the sky completely darken as they grew closer to the plantation.

As Robert turned the bus down the entrance to the property, the riders were awestruck as the building came into full view. In front of them, and getting closer with each turn of the wheels, sat The Magnolia Plantation. As the members of the tour took in its image, Robert gave them an overview of the building and property.

"Built in 1823 by Bernard Blanc, the Magnolia served as one of the largest Sugar Plantations in the south. It struggled in its early years due to droughts and mismanagement, however, the plantation boomed and expanded in the 1850s.

"Victoria Honoré inherited the property from her husband Charles Blanc when he died in 1857, just a few years before the start of the Civil War. For those of you who may have taken one of the other tours or had a history teacher who was a football coach, don't buy an ounce of the malarkey that they may have tried to tell you. The war was about Slavery. Some of those other tours focus so much on trying to charm visitors with Southern Fantasy and Margaret Mitchell fan fiction that they themselves believe it."

The comment received a few scattered chuckles throughout the bus before Robert brought it to a stop in front of the building.

"Welcome to The M agnolia, l adies a nd gentlemen. I'll give you a few minutes to stretch your legs, take some pictures, and then your guide, Ms. Jayne Humboldt, will meet us out here to get your tour started," Robert informed them as he opened the door.

The members of the tour disembarked from the bus, gathering outside. Brian watched as Lois and her friends took selfies together with the building serving as their backdrop.

Lucinda leaned over to her brother, stating, "You know this is fucked up, right?"

"What?" Brian asked.

"The fact that they are giggling and bullshitting where some of our ancestors were beaten and raped. Maybe you should ask her if she wants to visit Auschwitz for your honeymoon."

"Luci, ok... you took a class or two in college, I get it," he responded, frustrated.

"Brian!" Lois motioned for him. "Take a picture of us together!"

"Sure," he said, grabbing her phone. He held the phone up, pointing it at the group. "I'm going to see if I can get most of the building in the shot. All I am getting is the porch."

As he tracked them in the frame, Brian saw an image emerge in an upstairs window. He looked closer at the screen. It was the face of an older woman. Her hair was long and gray. Her eyes were sunken. Brian locked his eyes with hers before she vanished. The sudden disappearance of the woman gave him goosebumps.

Stepping back, Brian's foot landed on an uneven area of the driveway. His ankle rolled, causing him to fall to the ground and on to his side. Stumbling and trying to avoid injuring himself in the fall, he dropped Lois' phone to the ground.

Lucinda and Marcus grabbed Brian's arm, helping him to his feet.

"Damn dude, I thought you were trying out some new dance move," Marcus chuckled.

"Dance?" Lucinda retorted, "Brian is the only person in our family with a chronic case of no rhythm."

Lois jogged over; her action was more of a show than actual compassion. Seeing that Brian was upright, her concern turned to her phone whose cracked screen twinkled back at her. She picked it up off of the ground as if it were a dying pet. Lois pushed the power button, illuminating the screen. She stared at the distorted image for a few seconds before accepting what had happened.

"I should have just asked someone else to take the picture," she said as she walked back over to her friends.

"I'm fine, by the way," Brian said, dusting himself off.

5

Robert called the tourists to the front of the house with a wide grin and cheerful demeanor.

"Again, ladies and gentlemen, I want to welcome you to the Magnolia. We are very fortunate tonight as the tour will fully live up to its title. As you can see from the sky, we have a full moon above. In case you were wondering, you shouldn't worry about werewolves or any other fictional monsters w hile w e are on the grounds... besides, we are more of a vampire town, anyway." A few members of the crowd chuckled.

"Now, ladies and gentlemen, I will turn you over to my colleague, Jayne Humboldt, your guide for the evening," Robert said as he motioned to a slender, dark-haired woman emerging from the building.

"Good evening, all. I am Jayne Humboldt, and I am a senior historian with the Louisiana Parks and Archives Department. I want to thank you all for taking this tour and engaging with the history of this land. Before we begin, are there any questions?"

Scanning the crowd, Jayne was relieved that no hands were raised. She always cherished tours that did not start off with questions. It resulted in the tours being more focused on the content of the building, its history, and the related events rather than someone's preconceived notions and ideas about the site. As she moved her head from left to right, she saw one hand, slightly raised.

"Yes?"

"Ms. Humboldt?" Brian hesitantly asked.

"Jayne, please," she responded

"Are there any other tour groups on the property?"

"No. Your group is the only one booked and the last one scheduled for this evening."

"Oh. I just thought that I saw someone in the window by the balcony upstairs."

"Well, I am the only one here. I come out with the morning tour and stay on the property throughout the day and leave with the night tours when we have them. There's no use in me travelling back and forth, plus it gives me the opportunity to work on my research while here. This home has a very rich history, and I hope all of you enjoy your time here.

"If there are no other questions, we can begin the tour. I want to stress to you all the importance that you respect this home and the history within its walls. As an historian, we often find ourselves uncovering uncomfortable truths that were buried by time and individuals. Please enjoy your time here but be mindful that this place is one of both joy and of sorrow," Jayne said, motioning for the group to join her on the porch.

She led the men and women through the entryway telling them about the construction of the home, the style, and the various renovations completed. Each bit of information provided the tour guests with a generous background on the home's place in history. Jayne walked the group through the kitchen, discussing the eating habits and elaborate meals that would be prepared for special occasions. Jayne led the group into the ballroom enchanting them with stories of elegance and opulence. She detailed the romantic affairs and m arriages that b egan in that v ery room.

Lois, enamored with the decorative

features and size of the ballroom, leaned into Brian, remarking that this would be a great place for them to exchange vows. Her offer was not received in the fashion she had hoped so she raised her hand, gaining the attention of Jayne.

"Yes, ma'am?" Jayne asked.

"Jayne, do the owners of this home rent out this venue for weddings and receptions?"

"No. The owners of this property want this building to serve as an educational tool and as a way for people to better understand the circumstances and reality of the institution of slavery in the United States, especially considering how that sad reality and brutal chapter of this nation's history has been overshadowed by the myths we have allowed people to believe."

Marcus, under his breath, scoffed and remarked, "What kind of stupid motherfuckers would want to get married at a slave plantation?"

Lucinda, catching his comment, whispered to him. "I think we both already know at least one." Jayne continued walking the guests through the home, stopping to admire the library.

Marcus interrupted her as she began detailing the history of the room, "Excuse me, Jayne... the corridor we just passed through, what do those doors lead to?"

Jayne, caught off guard, replied, "Oh, my apologies. That is the wine room. The room itself holds well over five hundred bottles and spirits."

"Is there anything in there right now?" Donna asked.

"Oh yes. The family keeps that room locked and does not include it in the tour because of the collection they have built. Some of the wines are older than this home. The family still deposits bottles from time to time. When the house is not in use for tours, they sometimes come here to enjoy a drink or two in peace."

Jayne quickly returned the tour's attention to the library informing them of the rare items, first editions of books, original maps, artwork, and artifacts that the family had discovered or purchased. Several of the guests found themselves captivated by the world that had been created around them in the room. With a few exceptions, the group was fully engaged in the literary paradise that had floor to ceiling shelving filled with books, relics, and pictures. One framed picture holding the image of a little black boy and a little white girl, arm in arm, caught the attention of Daphne.

"Lois! Brian! Look. These two look like you!" she said as she called them over to inspect the picture.

"How cute, babe," Lois remarked.

Brian approached the shelf and looked more closely at the image, taking the time to read the wording at the bottom.

Isaiah and Rose: Slave Children from New Orleans.

Jayne's attention was drawn to the small group that had assembled around the photograph.

"Oh yes. This photo is one of many from abolitionist publications prior to and during the Civil War. It was a way to get Northerners more fully behind and invested in abolitionist efforts by showing the humanity of the enslaved. It was much easier to ignore what was taking place in the slaveholding states so long as you couldn't put a face to it. Hearing the stories and firsthand experiences of people like Frederick Douglass was one thing, but seeing children suffer in this system really made it hard for people to turn a blind eye to what was taking place. It forced people to ask why children would be permitted to suffer this indignity and inhumanity. For some, images like this were all that it would take for them to get off the fence with respect to the institution of slavery.

Calista interjected, "Is it true that the Blanc family were part of the abolition movement here in the south? I've been doing some research but haven't been able to find anything substantial to demonstrate their role in the antislavery movement."

"Well, if you find anything, please let me

know. There has been very little documentation to support the theories that they were participants. Unfortunately, understanding the Blanc family's public statements and some of the letters that have survived, not to mention their dependence on the system of slavery for wealth and political power, it is hard to believe that this would have been possible. Charles Blanc died shortly after marrying his wife, Victoria. She was sixteen at the time they exchanged vows. He was forty–seven," Jayne informed the group.

Murmurs and shock were expressed by the tourists at receiving this information.

"Gross," Donna blurted.

"Yeah. Kind of like your dad and his new trophy wife," Daphne laughed.

After spending a few more moments in the library, allowing the tour to absorb more of the character of the room, Jayne led them into the adjoining area.

"Ladies and gentlemen, this is the family room. The furniture and fixtures are all as they were in the nineteenth century. Aside from the wiring, this room is as it would have been when the original owners occupied it. This room was used, primarily, as a receiving room for guests. Aside from that, the room was used as a makeshift hospital where injured soldiers were treated for minor wounds during the Civil War.

I should have mentioned this earlier, but the kitchen was used as a surgery. If the injuries were severe enough and someone died, their remains were stored just outside of this house in what affectionately became known as 'The Bone Shack' where they stayed until they could be buried or shipped home for interment." Jayne pointed through the window to a small building that sat in the distance. "It had served as a carriage house up until the war."

After a few photos of the room and questions, Jayne continued the tour, leading the guests back into the foyer by the stairs. After taking a few steps up, she pointed out an imposing portrait with a figure staring down at them.

"I present to you, Victoria Blanc, mistress of The Magnolia Plantation, and her cat, Bishop."

The tourists pointed their cameras and phones at the portrait intending to capture the image as a memento of their journey to the Magnolia. The image was an intimidating presence. Victoria's hazel eyes followed her guests around the room, unsettling several of those on the tour. The detail in the painting gave her the appearance of life. Guests remarked at how the image looked as though it were breathing. Despite the discomfort it created, the portrait revealed the beauty of this woman. She appeared young. Her hair was dark and long, the only break from the dark color was accomplished with the placement of a Magnolia bloom in her right hand. Her left hand placed on the back of her black and gray cat offered a bit of comfort in contrast to the sense that they were being watched.

As the tourists admired the portrait, Jayne continued discussing the aspects of the room, the type of wood in the stairs, and the tapestries on the wall. Brian continued his focus as the other members of the tour walked up the stairs, arriving on to the second-floor landing.

"Remarkable," he said in admiration.

"I've been studying up on this woman," Calista said as she saw that his attention was still on the image of Victoria. "She is quite impressive. I discovered that she made it a condition of her marriage to Charles Blanc that he emancipate his slaves. When his father, Bernard Blanc, heard about her demand, he interjected."

"What happened?" Brian inquired.

"She poisoned him," Calista said in a serious tone.

"Holy shit! Did he die?" Brian asked

"No. Apparently she had a voodoo priestess make a potion that caused him to lose his mind. He was seen running through the streets of New Orleans completely nude. The state awarded his son sole ownership and control over all the property. Bernard died not long after. Charles and Victoria were married a few months later. He died shortly after they wed from cholera. Victoria ended up getting all of the property, land, slaves, and money," Calista continued.

"So, did she free the slaves?" he followed.

"There was nothing showing that she initially freed them en masse. There were some enslaved people that she freed or allowed to buy their freedom, but her land, wealth, and number of slaves expanded up until the Civil War."

"Why did she go back on a condition that she wanted?" Brian probed.
"Maybe she got corrupted by the money? Not sure. But after Reconstruction ended, she killed herself. Maybe she couldn't deal with all of the changes that had taken place."

Their conversation was interrupted by Jayne's voice cutting through the momentary pause. Brian and Calista rejoined the group as they began proceeding through the rooms on the second floor. Each room offered its own charm and individuality. Walking through them made the guests feel as though they had traveled through time.

As they exited and approached the landing once more, Jayne, in dramatic fashion walked over to the French doors that they had passed when first arriving on the second floor. She grabbed a handle on each, pushing the doors open, reciting lines that she found herself stating countless times before.

"The *pièce de resistance!* A banquet for the eyes... I present to you, ladies and gentlemen, the master bedroom of Victoria Blanc."

The group was more awestruck than when they saw the image of her. The room was filled with color. The rugs, tapestries, drapes, and murals on the walls were breathtaking. There was still a faint aroma of jasmine and lavender in the air. The canopy bed placed against the wall to the right was immense. It looked as though it were built for five people to sleep comfortably. The linens were a medley of color: purple, gold, lavender, and blue adorned the bed and the chaise lounges placed in the room. The room sprung with life, giving the impression that it had waited on its guests for the opportunity to finally present its splendor to the world.

Jayne jokingly warned those on the tour to not fall in love with the room as she explained that trying to acquire the type of silk, linen, and fabrics to replicate the look of just the bedding would cost a small fortune. Trudy, who had been fairly unimpressed through much of the tour, mustered up the ability to ask a question.

"Does anyone actually live here?"

"In this house? No," Jayne responded. "In fact, no one has lived in this house since the death of Madame Blanc. Her family set up a trust to oversee the house with the requirement that it is not to be sold nor can anyone occupy the home. It wasn't until thirty years ago that the trust decided to open the home to the public for the sake of educational tours. Aside from that, the only people allowed in are family members and caretakers."

Brian let out a sigh of relief. "That's probably who I saw earlier."

"Pardon?"

"When we were outside, I saw someone in an upstairs window. It was probably one of the caretakers coming in to clean up between tours."

"That's not possible. The caretakers only come on non–tour days, and I am the only one who has been on the property today."

"Are you sure?"

"Yes. I come with the morning tours and stay when they leave. I am here for the afternoon and evening tours when we have them. Before I ride back with the evening tour, I lock everything up and shut the lights off. All in all, I am probably on the property twelve to fourteen hours when we have a full schedule."

Eli spoke up. "You have the run of the house, all day? I'd go mad in a place like this if I were by myself."

"Well, it allows me to get a good amount of work done between tours, but enough about that."

Jayne walked the group through the room, allowing them to inspect the dressers, vanity, chaise lounges, and ornate patterns that decorated the walls. The size of the chamber rivaled the ballroom. They were then ushered through to the connected room which Jayne informed them had served as a nursery on more than a few occasions. As the group filed into the nursery, Jayne opened the doors leading to the balcony.

"Ladies and gentlemen, this balcony, just as much of the rest of the house, is filled with history. When Union troops arrived in this area, Victoria Blanc allowed them to use this building as a command center and as a makeshift hospital, as I stated earlier. This balcony allowed Union forces to scout potential enemy positions and encampments. If you look in the distance, you can see all the way to downtown New Orleans. The advantage of this balcony is that it wraps around the building following the same layout as the porch underneath us. When this served as a working plantation, the balcony allowed one to observe any of the enslaved laborers and overseers. Please take some time to enjoy the view and breathe in the evening air."

Guests walked around the balcony. The soles of their shoes connecting with the boards made a rhythmic sound. The croaking of the frogs in the distance matched the intensity of the slats of wood creaking under the weight of the tour guests. Calista, while the other guests took photos, leaned over the balcony to discover what they could see in the distance, or engaged in conversation, stood still. She was uneasy. She wanted to ask Jayne a question but was unsure of how to approach the topic. She sunk her head down and slowly approached Jayne who was checking her phone.

"Is this where her body was found?" she warily asked.

"I beg your pardon?" Jayne responded in disbelief.

"Victoria... is this where it happened?" Calista asked while leaning against the balcony railing outside of the master bedroom.

"I'm not sure of what you are talking about."
The other members of the tour caught pieces of the conversation and had their attention focused on the two women.

"Whose body?" Eli asked.

"What is she talking about?" Margaret asked.

"That girl said something about Victoria's

body. What happened?" Eric inquired.

Jayne was overwhelmed with questions about the death of the homeowner. She was flustered and her skin became flush with color. She didn't know how to approach the subject. There was little she knew about it. For the first time in years, she was confronted about the death of Victoria.

"Honestly, I don't know. Her children were told about her death while they were off in school. Some of the people that were working on the land, hired laborers to manage the fields after the war, found her body hanging from the balcony. When her children were notified, they all were so disturbed by their mother dying here that they were not comfortable with the idea of ever living in the house, but they also couldn't sell the home because of all the work she put into it."

"Why didn't you tell us about that in the beginning? That gives us even more interest in the house and the history here," Marcus said, excitedly.

"As I stated before, the family wanted the house to serve as an educational tool not as someone's fodder for ghost stories or legends surrounding the south."

6

Robert stood outside, enjoying a cigarette in the moonlight. He listened to the frogs singing in the distance. He loved the peace and tranquility that came with southern nights. Where some found the humidity and bugs to be a nuisance, he viewed them as part of the character and charm of the south.

He strolled leisurely down the tree–lined gravel road that served as the only way in and the only way out of the property. Robert had been on this land for hundreds of tours and always took the time to walk down the gravel road while the tour was being conducted inside of the house. The walk down the road gave him time away from members of the tour and permitted him to be alone with his thoughts.

As he leaned up against one of the trees, he took a long drag off of his cigarette and looked at his watch, gauging the amount of time that he would have to himself before being needed back at the bus.

Robert spun his keys around his middle finger as he leisurely walked back to the bus. The gravel crunched under his feet with each step. The sound reverberated down the road creating a slight echo. Robert chuckled to himself as he thought about the best way to silently walk back to the bus. He thought about making a game of it trying to imagine himself as a ninja approaching his target. He slid his feet smoothly across the gravel to make his arrival as stealthy as possible. Robert shifted his hips and his weight with each movement. Cigarette in his mouth, and keys in his hand, he grew quieter with each step.

Proud of his accomplishment, Robert threw forward a powerful karate chop. He stood, holding his attack pose, exhaling cigarette smoke from his nostrils. In the quiet of that dark road, he heard a rustle in the brush. Robert feared the worst as he looked at his outstretched, empty hand.

"Fuck!" he uttered as the cigarette dropped from his mouth. Robert walked over to the source of the sound. Beads of sweat formed on his brow, trickling down his face. The crunching of the gravel ceased as he reached the dirt shoulder of the road. He pulled out his cell phone, using the light in his search for the keys. Robert pointed the light into the brush, hoping to find a small flicker.

Nothing bounced any measure of light back at him. All he illuminated were plants and dirt. Not finding the keys was not an option. He proceeded into the brush further. He shined the light from the phone, waving it from left to right. His eye caught a short flash of light. Robert's heart fluttered at seeing his keys resting on the ground at the base of a tree. He knelt, reaching forward to grasp them. Robert held them tightly in his hand as he jogged back to the road. Making his way through the dark, suffocating b rush, his foot caught a tree root forcing him to lose his balance. He crashed to the ground.

Rather than check for any injuries, he immediately inspected his hand. The keys were still in his possession.

Robert pushed away from the ground. As his arms became fully extended, he was met by two yellow eyes. Robert slowly stepped backwards, before quickly turning to run from the beast. Panicked, he ran into a thick oak tree, hitting his head. He stumbled back to the road, his head throbbing.

Losing his balance, he fell to the ground. Robert struggled to stand. Holding his hand to his forehead, Robert was disoriented. His heart raced. Panic set in as Robert's feet struck the gravel. His feet dragged along the ground. His breathing shortened and his vision blurred. Robert clutched his chest, falling to the ground. The lights of the house danced in the distance. His eyes closed as he reached out his hand toward the house. The keyring fell to the ground as he lost the strength to hold on.

7

Jayne led the members of the tour down the stairs and through the entrance. Departing the building, she thanked them all for attending the tour. They walked down the steps from the porch, approaching the bus. As the group made their trek to their transport. Jayne locked the doors and checked the perimeter as she did each night at the end of a tour.

Marcus, being the first to arrive tried entering the bus in vain. The door did not budge. He pressed his face to the glass seeing no one inside. He knocked on the door to no avail.

"What's the hold up?" Eli asked.

"The door's locked. Anyone see the driver?" Marcus responded.

Frustrated, Margaret interjected, "He was here when we left. Anyone have his number?"

"Give him a minute. He's probably off taking a piss or something before we head back," Marcus responded.

"I'm not waiting out here forever," Lois grumbled as she crossed her arms.

"Maybe you can get on your broom," Lucinda said under her breath.

Eli looked around to see if he could catch Robert coming around the building or down the road and found no sign of him. He pulled out his cigarettes, offering one to Anne.

"Guess this would be a good time to get a smoke while we wait."

"Seriously. Where is this guy? We have an early flight tomorrow, and I didn't b other packing yet," Margaret said, looking around for Robert.

Eric looked at his watch. "Best case scenario is that we get back to the hotel by midnight which should give us a few hours to sleep before catching the shuttle in the morning." Eli groaned in response to Eric's news.

The tour members stood outside of the building watching as lights turned off from the building. Jayne emerged from the front door. She approached the crowd outside of the bus.

"Everyone ready to go?"

"We definitely are, but we have a minor issue," Marcus said.

Jayne looked puzzled.

"No driver," he said, pointing into the bus.

"Oh. Robert is normally here at the end of the tour. I'm usually the one everyone is waiting for. Let me give him a ring," she offered, pulling out her cell phone. After entering his number, the phone rang until she was met with his voicemail prompt. Jayne nervously left a message inquiring about his whereabouts. She felt the eyes of the crowd bearing down on her.

As she ended the call, she looked up trying to reassure the guests. Jayne expressed that it should only be a short wait before Robert returned, apologizing to them. She felt uneasy and anxious. After all the tours she had conducted over the years with Robert as her driver, this was the first time that he was not waiting in the bus. Quelling the concerns and unease of the crowd was the only way that she could deal with her own worries.

8

The dark sky offered little consolation to everyone as its ominous presence made them more fearful and apprehensive as to what may be lurking in the shadows.

Marcus leaned up against the bus remarking how he wished his parents had allowed him to be a juvenile delinquent rather than having pushed him into academic pursuits. He joked with Brian about how he would have learned something more useful like boosting cars and picking locks if he had stayed on that path. He noted how much more helpful those skills are as opposed to memorizing the Pythagorean theory. Brian made the mistake of laughing.

"This isn't funny, Brian. We are stuck out

here. Where is the driver, huh? Nothing about this is funny. My friends showed up drunk. You and Marcus are just goofing off. I just wanted to have a nice getaway for all of us to enjoy before we get married. The only bright spot is that your sister has been here!"

Lucinda immediately thought about how ridiculous bringing her into the conversation was. She wanted nothing to do with Lois and was only there to convince her brother to break off the engagement.

"Thanks, Luci," Lois stated in a seemingly genuine tone.

"Sure," Lucinda replied through a forced smile.

Lightning flashed overhead, disrupting the general quiet that the group enjoyed as they waited for Robert's return or at least a phone call from him to Jayne. The loud rumble that followed shook the ground.

"I sure hope he gets here soon," Margaret said anxiously.

"I just hope we don't have to travel in that when we fly home in the morning," Anne added.

Jayne dialed Robert's number again receiving no response.

A whistling breeze pushed its way toward them. The chill of the air unsettling them even more. Several members of the group look up to witness the clouds fully embrace the sky, shrouding the stars and moonlight. Drops of rain fell from the sky lightly and then increased in speed and size.

"This is not happening," Lois grunted as she covered her head.

Jayne, surprised at how the events of the night had escalated, ushered everyone to the house. After unlocking the doors, everyone rushed behind her into the foyer. Jayne again offered a stream of apologies to everyone. She was embarrassed at how the past few moments had unfolded.

Where is Robert? She thought to herself. *Where the hell is he?*

Seeing the need to keep everyone calm and maintain control, Jayne called the tour office. She hoped that Terrance was still there, but she knew better. He had never been at the office when she came back with the late tours. Her fears were confirmed. There was no answer on the office line. The rain helped hide the perspiration that beaded up on her face as she worried more about what course of action to take.

"Ladies and gentlemen, my apologies, but there is no answer at the tour office. We will just have to wait a bit longer. Hopefully, it will not be that much longer, but I guess the good news is that you get to experience an extended tour," she said with a nervous smile. "Please feel free to walk around the house. My apologies for the inconvenience."

Initially, there was some grumbling and murmuring, but some of the attendees decided to make the best of the situation. Calista, who had enjoyed the tour, took the opportunity to consume more of the home's history. She walked through the building inspecting everything more closely. The house was more alive to her as she viewed the decorative features more deeply. She took her time viewing the molding, carvings, and the weaving of the rugs. The pattering of the rain and blowing of the wind offered a soundtrack that guided her back to the ballroom.

The others remained gathered near the front entrance as they awaited Robert's arrival and the departure of the rain. Marcus looked through the window and was more than dissatisfied with the view. He knew the rain would not come to an end anytime soon.

"So, is there a TV or something in here... or something we can do while we wait?" he asked.

"The entertainment is fairly limited in the home. There is a chess set and books in the library, of course," Jayne informed him. "The only modern conveniences the family added are the bathrooms, plumbing for the kitchen, and the security system.

"Really?"

"Yes. No one has lived in this house since Victoria Blanc died. Her children didn't feel comfortable living in the house after her death."

"Why is that?" Margaret asked.

"There are rumors that because she never specified who would get the house, they all agreed that none of them would outright own the home or live in it, so they decided to keep the home as collective property."

"How progressive," Brian added.

"Yeah, if this house were in my family, we would have probably cut each other's throats to get it. Last man standing would take over," Eric joked.

"Jesus, what do you do for a living?" Brian asked.

"Sales," he replied.

Jayne continued, "The children passed the house down through the family with the caveat that no one lay claim to the house for themselves and that none of them can live in the house. This tour is probably the latest anyone has ever stayed in the home. No one has occupied the home or even stayed overnight since Victoria. The family didn't want the house to go to waste so they permitted leasing of the land for agricultural purposes and deemed the house to be used for educational endeavors like tours and academic research."

"What about weddings?" Lois asked.

"Absolutely not," Jayne responded.

"I don't see why not. This would be a perfect place for one," Lois insisted.

"Jesus Christ! Do you want people picking cotton in the background, so it is truly authentic?" Lucinda blurted, surprising Lois. She was even more shocked that Brian said nothing to his sister in response. Marcus shot a "thumbs up" to Lucinda, showing his approval of her response.

Jayne interjected, "There are many things that occurred on this property. The enslavement of people was one of the darkest chapters of this home's history and one of the aspects that the owners do not wish to have whitewashed or romanticized. After the war, Victoria Blanc became an advocate for suffrage and political rights for the free black community in this area."

"And that's why she was murdered," Calista said in a cold tone, emerging from the corridor.

"I'm sorry, but there isn't much, if anything to support that," Jayne said, befuddled. "Wait, what?" Lucinda asked, intrigued. "The death of Victoria is dubious. She wasn't a very popular woman with the white community for a few reasons. When the war came here, she willingly hosted Union troops and continued to do so during Reconstruction.

During that time, she advocated for voting rights of Black residents. Some have theorized that she was murdered, especially in the Black community. Unfortunately, there were no suspects and no one willing to come forward. Even the family did not want to press the issue, so they allowed her death to be recorded as a suicide. She was found hanging from her balcony by workers coming to tend to the sugar and rice fields one morning," Jayne added.

"Why didn't you tell us about this on the tour?" Brian asked.

"In my official capacity it would be inappropriate to discuss speculation, especially if the family doesn't express their desire for it to be included, but I guess all of you are getting the bonus features of this tour given our circumstances. Professionally, my research has been focusing on Victoria and coming to terms with what took place during her life and what led to her death. Being the way things are in this part of the world and dealing with the people that were around during that period, it has been less than ideal when trying to find sources to support some of my theories."

Calista, having taken a keen interest in the home and researching Victoria Blanc, felt validated for the hours she spent digging through archives and public records.

The rain outside increased in intensity. Jayne checked her phone again to see if there were any messages. Her phone lacked any indications of messages or missed calls.

Lightning flashed outside, magnifying the amount of light in the house. The rumble of the thunder instantly followed the illumination. The windows rattled and the decorations shook. The guests were startled by the force that nature displayed. The group sat in silence and awe as the electrical performance played out. The flashes of light were so brilliant and powerful that none of them noticed the power at The Magnolia had ceased.

9

The break in the lightning left the group stranded in darkness. Jayne turned on the flashlight to her phone, illuminating the room.

"Is everyone okay?" she asked, panning the phone around the room. The group's response was a mix of confusion, disappointment, and unease. "We have some candles in the kitchen and some lanterns that we could use while we wait. Does anyone have a lighter?"

"Wait, for what? We've been here for nearly an hour!" Lois snapped. "I'm calling an Uber."

She unlocked her phone making a request through the app. There were no cars visible in the area on the map.

"Nothing?" She scoffed. "Not a single car

shows as available on the app."

"Yeah, I guess the poor schmoes don't want to risk their lives to come out here in a thunderstorm," Marcus responded. Lois pursed her lips, the light of her phone making her look more ominous.

"Follow me, everyone," Jayne called out as she held her lit phone over her head. She proceeded to the kitchen where each of the members of the group were given a thick beige candle and matches. Handing them out, Jayne passed on instructions, "Everyone, if you would, please light the candles, lanterns and wall sconces on this floor. I do not think that the family would concern themselves too much if we were to make use of them, given our circumstances."

"Yeah, not a problem. I'll take the library. Marcus still owes me a rematch in chess," Brian joked. "Babe, want to come?" he asked, turning to Lois on his way out of the room.

"No, I'll just wait here."

Brian and Marcus walked off with Lucinda closely behind.

"I think I'd be more comfortable waiting this out with the two of you instead of hanging back with Lois and her friends," she whispered to Marcus.

Calista returned to the ballroom. The grand piano sitting near the windows intrigued her when the tour first entered the room. She took the opportunity presented to play a song or two. Calista thought that a bit of music might be necessary and welcome. She lit the candles on the sconces and in the candle holder on top of the piano before sitting down on the bench. There were no sheets of music present. The only hope she had was that she could remember something other than *Chopsticks*.

She placed her fingers on the keys, straining to see her hand placement in the dim light. All the lessons and instruction she had received as a child flooded her thoughts. There was no clarity with any of the messages. She pushed her fingers on to the keys and was met with sour notes. It was clear that, despite the impeccable condition the piano was in, it had not been tuned in a long while. Embarrassed and disappointed, Calista sat there, enjoying the solitude and emptiness the room provided. Despite being the lone person in the ballroom, she did not feel alone.

Eli and Eric, seeking an opportunity to explore more of the house, used the ruse of lighting candles in the hallway to make their way up the stairs to the second level. They gingerly walked up the stairs trying to avoid any creaks or noise as their feet contacted the steps. Having successfully made it to the landing, the two men directed their attention to the main bedroom.

"Holy shit, man," Eli said in a hushed tone. "This is even cooler in the dark. There are some really spooky vibes coming from this place."

"Yeah, this is where that girl said it happened, right?" Eric asked.

"Yeah," Eli's eyes widened as he looked in the direction of the balcony.

Eric approached the wide doors that led outside. Looking back, he noticed Eli had not moved from his spot.

"Dude, we've already been up here. Do you think that Victoria is out there just waiting for us?"

"No. It's not that. I just got a weird feeling in here... like someone is watching us," Eli said nervously.

Eric looked behind him, seeing a part of Victoria's portrait over his shoulder. The mix of shadow and flickering candlelight made her image look even more intimidating. His eyes widened and his mouth was agape.

"What is it?" Eli asked.

"Behind you," he whispered. "She's... I can see her. Don't move."

Eli was frozen with fear. Eric slowly approached him. He reached out his hand, touching Eli's shoulder. He gripped him tighter and turned him around. Seeing the image behind him, Eli was relieved.

"You really are an asshole," Eli stated in response to the ruse.

"Don't make it so easy then. Eli, there is no one up here but us. Everyone else is downstairs. Besides, I just had a great idea of how we could fuck with the girls. They are probably terrified right now with the lights going out and the storm raging outside... not to mention that one chick on the tour was talking about that lady dying here. Houses like this have all types of secret shit. Tell you what, hide behind the curtains over there on the wall. I'll hide over here, and we'll make some noise. When they come up, we'll jump out and scare the shit out of them. They don't know we are up here, so it's perfect," Eric plotted. Eli didn't look convinced. Seeing his lukewarm reception to the idea, Eric reminded Eli about all the pranks that Margaret had pulled on them back at the office.

Smiling, Eli agreed, thinking about the joy he would have in finally being able to exact his revenge on her. Margaret prided herself in being unprankable, all the while leaving fake voicemails or embarrassing her coworkers with elaborate tricks and ruses. He thought and quickly turned to Eric stating, "You get behind the curtains. I'll climb under the bed. We make some noise and call her upstairs. When she gets close to me, I'll grab her legs. With any luck, we'll get her to piss herself."

Margaret, Trudy, and Anne sat in the dining room at the candlelit table. While Trudy and Anne fumbled with their phones and updating their social media, Margaret fought off sleep, her head bobbing as she refrained from the call to rest.

An alert flashed on Anne's phone informing her of flash floods in the area.

She chuckled as she showed the information to Trudy.

"This evening couldn't get more perfect, could it?" Trudy said sarcastically.

"Jayne," Anne called over to the kitchen.

"Yes?"

"Is this an issue?" she asked, walking into the kitchen, showing her phone to Jayne. Looking over the weather alert, Jayne released a frustrated sigh.

"I'm afraid so. That was the one thing I was worried about when the rain came in so suddenly. This area is prone to flooding. The road, more than likely, is washed out."

"Meaning?"

"Meaning that we aren't going anywhere even if Robert were to walk through that door right now. Not to mention, no taxi, Uber, or Lyft is going to come out here given the road conditions."

Margaret sat comfortably in her chair at the dining table with her chin resting on her hand.

"*Margaret,*" an eerie voice called.
She looked up and saw Trudy with her earbuds in, playing on her phone.

"Trudy, did you say something?" There was no response, only the continued attention paid to her phone.

"*Margaret,*" the voice called out again.

She looked over her shoulder, only seeing the candlelit foyer that led to the stairs. Margaret rose and followed the call. She turned, looking up the staircase which held only one lit candle.

"*Margaret, I'm waiting for you,*" the voice creepily stated.

The steps creaked under her as she walked forward.

"*Margaret,*" the voice said, stretching out her name.

"You idiots better stop screwing around," she called out.

"*We have something to show you, Margaret.*"

Margaret hurried up the stairs, her steps louder than before. She stood at the landing, waiting for the voice to call again.

"Ma'am," Jayne called from the foyer. "You shouldn't be up there now. It's best that we all wait down here together."

"I heard someone up here," Margaret responded as she walked away through the door to the bedroom. Jayne followed up the stairs.

Margaret scanned the room, looking for anything. Her search was made more difficult as the dimly lit room allowed all shapes to run together. Nothing stood out.

"I know you are in here," Margaret declared. She walked over to a set of drapes running her hands across them, flinging them open. Nothing met her other than the window they had been covering. She walked over to another set and was met with the same result.

Jayne emerged at the doorway, watching as Margaret continued her performance. She flung open another set of drapes finding Eric standing behind them with his hands covering his mouth, stifling his laughter.

"Found you. Nice try." Margaret smiled.

"Yeah, yeah. No one can get Margaret the Magnificent," he said, rolling his eyes.

"Okay. You've had your fun, now please return downstairs," Jayne called out to them.

Eli, still under the bed, looked and waited for Margaret's feet to appear near where he was hiding.

"Come on," he whispered to himself.

Her white shoes came to a stop next to where he lay in wait while Margaret spoke with Jayne from across the room. Eli launched his hand forward, forcefully grasping her ankle and growling for extra measure. Caught off guard, Margaret screamed, stumbling toward the fireplace. She collapsed to the floor, inches away from the hearth. The impact of her body forced the shotgun sitting above the mantle to fall.

The weapon hit the floor, discharging on impact. Jayne froze in place as the barrels stared her down. It was the last thing she would see.

10

The gunshot, masked by the thunder, traveled through the house before Jayne's body collapsed to the floor. Eli, Eric, and Margaret looked on in horror and disbelief. Anne, having followed behind Jayne, dropped to her knees outside of the room in shock.

"Oh my God! What did you do?" Eli yelled at Margaret, sliding his body from under the bed.

"Me? You! You scared the hell out of me! I didn't do anything. The gun fell off the wall!" Margaret screamed.

"We need to call someone," Eric offered.

"Check her pulse," Eli offered.

Angered, Eric bellowed, "What fucking pulse?"

Eli looked down as Eric knelt next to the body, holding his phone up to his ear. Jayne's head was nothing more than a mass of blood, tissue, and hair. Her face was distorted and unrecognizable. Having taken in a full view of Jayne's corpse, Eli, overcome with nausea, vomited in the fireplace.

Anne, gaining the courage to rise and walk into the room was greeted with a ghastly display. Jayne's body lay on the ground in a dark pool of blood. Margaret was pacing the room and muttering to herself. Eli was regurgitating uncontrollably. Eric was the only one of them who looked composed, despite kneeling next to Jayne's bloody body.

"Is she dead?" Anne nervously asked.

"No, she's auditioning for the role of corpse number one on *Law and Order*!" Eric responded.

"You don't need to be an asshole about it," Anne shot back.

Eric made a dismissive face at her as his call was finally answered.

"Yes, I need someone to..." he said to the dispatcher.

"*Please stay on the line, sir*," the dispatcher instructed. Eric, holding the phone to his ear, awaited the return of the dispatcher on the other end so they could send someone to the house. As the seconds passed, a hissing noise entered his ear before going silent. Pulling the phone away from his ear, he looked at the screen. A cold sweat formed on his brow as he read the message on the screen detailing the end of the call. Eric punched the numbers again, attempting to reach emergency services. The call failed to connect.

Eric put the phone back in his pocket before sitting down on the floor.

"I can't get anyone," Eric said with an aggrieved tone.

"What do you mean?" Eli said, spitting on the floor.

"I called and they put me on hold. I called back and I get nothing on the other end."

Anne pulled out her phone, offering it to Eric. He dialed 911. The call would not go through. Frustrated, he pushed the emergency services button on the phone, achieving the same result. Margaret and Eli found the same outcome with their attempts.

The four solemnly looked at each other, questioning what the next step should be.

"We need to go downstairs and let everyone else know what happened. Maybe one of their phones is working and we can call to get someone out here," Eric offered.

"We should at least cover her up before we go back downstairs," Margaret said, concerned.

"No. We shouldn't touch her," Eli said as he

spit the last bit of vomit out of his mouth, "and we definitely shouldn't touch that fucking gun."

11

Trudy sat comfortably alone in the dining room. The candles flickered and danced to the music that flowed through her earbuds. The few days she and her team had spent in New Orleans had been filled with anything but productivity. She found joy in being able to get away from work with a few others from her company whose idea of a work trip had nothing to do with professional development. The tour was the closest thing any of them had engaged in that could qualify as team building.

She stood up from the table. The flashes of lightning through the window intrigued her. She enjoyed the violence that nature made possible. Trudy grabbed her chair and moved it to the window so she could watch the storm while waiting for the opportunity to leave.

Lightning continued to flash in the distance. The thunder boomed. Th e trees swayed as the wind tossed them back and forth. Trudy focused her gaze on the action as it played out. She was awestruck as she bore witness to the fury on display.

The flickering of the flames on the candles created an annoying glare on the window that interrupted the tranquility that Trudy found in her admiration of the ferocity on the other side of the glass. She walked over to the table. Lowering her head, she exhaled over each candle, extinguishing their flame.

With the candlelight no longer disturbing her view, Trudy continued observing the swaying trees among the flashes of lightning. She removed her earbuds, fully taking in the soundscape.

Trudy opened the window, removing the barrier which obstructed her from being completely immersed in the experience. Extending her head through the opening, she inhaled deeply, smelling the fresh rain and air. The wind carried some of the rain toward her face. The cool droplets refreshed her skin. Pulling her head back, she rested her hands on the windowsill.

Taking another deep breath of the night air, lightning flashed, illuminating the entirety of the room. Trudy's chest tightened as the subsequent boom of thunder shook the room. The reverberations loosened the windowpane, slamming it down on both of her hands. The impact momentarily startling her, Trudy looked down to see her hands pinned under the frame. She pulled her fingers from under the window, inspecting them for injury. Her hands were free of damage.

She was relieved in discovering that her costume jewelry saved her hands from the impact of the window. Trudy stretched her fingers and shook her hands to return to a state of relaxation. Closing her eyes, she took another deep breath and counted down from ten as she exhaled the air.

10...9...8...7...6...5...4...3...2...1...

She opened her eyes and looked through the window again, watching the storm continue. The flashes of lightning continued. The rumbles followed. The trees swayed. The darkness of the room allowed her to be lulled by the actions outside. Placing her hands against the window, she pressed her face to the pane. Another bright flash emerged from the sky. In the illumination, Trudy saw a woman standing outside. As the light from the storm receded, the women disappeared. Another flash of light brought a return of the figure. Trudy saw her clearly. The woman held out her right arm, extending her hand toward Trudy. As the darkness returned, the woman's image departed.

"Get it together, Trudy," she said to herself.

Trudy regained her focus as she looked through the glass. There was nothing on the other side of the window other than the raging storm. She inched away from the sill. Stepping back, she could hear the faint sound of water dripping. Looking up to the ceiling, she feared the roof had begun to leak from the storm. She held out her hand in the darkness hoping to catch a drop to confirm her suspicion.

She slowly approached the source of the sound. The plips of water guided her. As she drew closer, the sound of the drops increased. Trudy held out her right hand, stretching it out in front of her as she stepped forward. She moved her arm to the left and right in vain, finding nothing wet nor the sensation of drops in her hand. The lightning continued flashing outside, giving momentary glimpses of the furniture and decorations staged in the room. The shadows created by the lightning distorted the room. Frustrated at not being able to find the source of the noise, she turned back to the window. The drips became louder. Trudy looked down at the windowsill. A pool of water collected near the edge and spilled onto the floor. Seeing the closed window puzzled Trudy.

Where was the water coming from?

Trudy ran her hands over her head. Nothing made sense. She touched the sill to confirm what her eyes were telling her. The cold water enveloped her hand as she placed it on the wood. Trudy wiped the water off on her shirt as she tried to rationalize what she experienced. She sat back down at the table, directing her attention to the playlist on her phone. As she scrolled through her collection, she felt dampness on her shoulder.

"Great... I guess I found the leak."

As she looked up to the ceiling again, she felt pressure build on her shoulders. Tilting her head back, she discovered the figure looming over her. Trudy could not see its face. Its hold of her tightened. The figure looked down upon her, opening its mouth.

"*You should not be here,*" it said in a hushed, raspy voice.

Trudy froze.

The gruff, feminine voice repeated, *'You should not be here.'*

Tears welled up in Trudy's eyes. Her lips quivering, she struggled to breathe. The figure, sensing her fear, released Trudy. Trudy shielded her mouth with both hands, gently sobbing and rocking back and forth in the chair. She watched as the figure drifted away, disappearing into the tapestry on the wall. Trudy breathed into her hands, the air passing through her fingers. Her eyes focused on the wall where the apparition departed. Her concentration was broken as Anne entered the room, sobbing erratically.

Trudy's gaze transferred to her friend as her concern changed from her recent experience to the well–being of her friend.

"Are you ok?" Trudy asked.

"She's ... dead..." Anne responded with stifled breath.

Trudy didn't know what to make of what she said. Momentarily, she thought that what she envisioned may have been in her imagination. Perhaps it had even been a result of fatigue. Maybe it was just being in the house that made her see things that were not there. Anne's statement confirmed to her that the concern was not imagined.

"You saw her too?"

"She's dead, Trudy."

"Where did you see her?"

"She's dead... on the floor... upstairs." She continued sobbing.

"What do you mean, on the floor?"

"We all went upstairs... and her head... her head just exploded."

"What?"

"Jayne. Jayne's dead, Trudy."

Confused, Trudy realized that they had different, unconnected experiences.

"What do you mean Jayne's dead?"

Anne sat down at the table, catching her breath. "Margaret went upstairs, and we followed her. Eric and Eli were screwing around up there and, I don't know what to make of it, but there was a loud boom, and her head was gone."

Trudy sat down next to her, rubbing her arm as she continued gathering herself. Anne placed her hands on her knees, letting out a deep breath. As she exhaled, Eli, Margaret, and Eric crossed through the threshold. Margaret wrung her hands before joining Anne and Trudy at the table. Eli's face was completely flushed. Eric looked dazed as he walked to the window, sitting on the ledge.

"What happened up there?" Trudy asked them.

Margaret, Eli, and Eric all sat in silence.

"Guys?"

Again, there was no response. The three of them could not even look in her direction. Trudy grabbed a match from the table, relighting the candles.

"What happened?" she asked, raising a candleholder. "Anne says that Jayne is dead."

Eric rubbed his head and ran his hands to the back of his neck.

"What happened?"

"I... I don't know. We were screwing around upstairs trying to scare Margaret, but when we did, an old shotgun fell from the wall and shot Jayne in the head."

Trudy's eyes widened.

Eli lifted his head. "It's true. She's dead."

Overcome with the shock of this news, Trudy had forgotten about her own encounter and sat back down asking, "What do we do?"

12

Raising her head from the piano, Calista watched the flashes of lighting dance off the ballroom walls. Walking around the room, she took in the history. She imagined the numerous celebrations that may have taken place within the walls. She sensed the pain inside of the walls who sought to have their stories heard. Calista ran her fingers across the wall as she walked. She had looked forward to visiting the Magnolia for years in the hopes of finding out more about the history of the home and Victoria Blanc.

Calista pored over volumes of documents and correspondence in the archives hoping to find out more about who Victoria really was. There were stories and countless rumors which spoke to the complicated nature of the woman. Calista wanted clarity and came to this house seeking it.

She continued walking the length of the room as the lightning provided the illumination needed to continue her trek. Her fingertips brushed along the textures of the wall. The grooves and impressions changed with each step. A cold feeling overcame Calista as she sensed the house touching her in return. She paused as the sensation became palpable. Turning her head, Calista looked behind herself, hoping that the feeling was in her head and driven by the paranoia of being alone in the room. Her eyes narrowed as she focused on her arm.

A dark hand wrapped around her wrist. Shocked, she pulled away. The hand gently released its grip and disappeared into the wall. Calista blinked her eyes, hoping her imagination was getting the better of her. Imagination or not, Calista's discomfort in the room increased. She needed to leave. The subtle laughter coming from the darkness enhanced her desire to depart. She backed away from the source, arriving at the door which led to the library.

Calista walked into the library, finding Marcus and Brian in a heated chess match. "Check," Marcus confidently chirped.

"Nah. Try again," Brian replied. "That's an

illegal move."

"The hell it is!"

"Yes. Knights can only move in an 'L' shape, not diagonally. How many times do we have to go through this?"

"Well, it works when you're not paying attention."

Brian grabbed the white knight, moving it back to its prior position. "There are rules for a reason. Without them, this game is no different than pickup basketball down at Grove Park."
Before Brian could continue, he caught Calista out of the corner of his eye, motioning for her to join them.

Marcus smiled warmly as she sat down next to them.

"So, find anything cool?"

The small beads of sweat on the back of her neck cooled and ran down her spine.

"Nope. Just a piano that has seen better days."

"You play?" Marcus asked.

"Oh. Just the basics... besides, it was way out of tune."

"Oh no. I mean chess. This guy is a stickler, and I'm sure he's tired of beating me."

"No, thanks. I never learned how."

"With that storm out there, it doesn't look like we're going anywhere anytime soon so we can give you a quick lesson." Marcus rose, offering his seat to her.

He joined Lucinda who was rigorously inspecting the bookshelves. She ran her fingers over countless volumes of texts, ledgers, and decorative items that filled the shelves.

"Anything interesting?" Marcus inquired.

"You mean other than this whole house?" She looked past Marcus at her brother to ensure he was busy. "I've been meaning to talk to you."

"Finally going to profess your undying love for me?" Marcus chuckled.

Lucinda snorted. "Right..."

"Look, I've talked to him... and believe me, I've been as much of a dick to Lois as I possibly could be, but it seems like they are set on getting married."

Brian continued giving Calista her introductory lesson. Seeing this, Lucinda leaned in closer to Marcus, lowering her voice.

"I don't know what his deal is. He doesn't seem to be happy with her, yet he won't call it off."

"Give him some time. I'm sure whatever spell she has over him will wear off sooner or later."

"Emphasis on sooner," Lucinda remarked.

"Got the hang of it?" Brian asked.

"I think so," Calista responded. The two

began alternating moves as they engaged in their match, Brian coaching as they played.

13

Lucinda continued combing through the shelves looking for something to occupy her time and attention. Her index finger dragged over a black leather–bound book with gold lettering. In the dimly lit room, the words were hard to decipher. Taking her phone out of her pocket, Lucinda held the illuminated screen next to the shelf.

1857

Lucinda retrieved the book from the shelf and flipped through the pages. Each page was filled with names and numbers. She quickly closed the book as the gravity of it hit her. The book was the property ledger for the plantation. Each name was someone whose life was measured in dollar value. Each individual on the pages had been denied their humanity.

Her stomach sank as she returned the book to its spot. Placing the ledger on the shelf, she was met with resistance as she attempted to slide the book into its designated position. Something obstructed the path. Lucinda fumbled as she stuck her hand between the volumes that rested to the left and the right of 1857's resting spot. Lucinda reached her hand into the gap. She felt something rough and hard. She reached further into the shelf grasping the object in the back of the bookcase. Lucinda gave it a stiff push, but it did not budge. Grasping it again, she pulled it toward her.

Clink

Lucinda feared that she had broken something in this ancient home. She concerned herself with the possibility of having to reimburse the caretakers for the cost of repairs. Before she could calculate the estimates in her head, Lucinda watched as the bookshelf slowly moved. There was a low, grinding noise as the shelf inched toward her.

Brian, Marcus, and Calista were all engaged in conversation, failing to notice the wall's motion. Had their attention been focused, they would have seen Lucinda as she walked down the corridor that had been concealed behind the wall of literature.

14

"So, what brought you out on the tour?" Brian asked.

"Oh, I just finally got some time away from school and work. You?" Calista responded.

"It was one of the activities that the hotel suggested, so we all decided to come out here before we leave in a couple of days."

The two continued playing and conversing before being interrupted by Marcus. Sitting next to them, he caught Calista's attention.

"I've been meaning to ask you. What is your interest in this place? I mean... you didn't strike me as a tourist or just someone with a passing curiosity... especially with some of the questions you asked on the tour."

Marcus inquired.

Calista sat back in her chair. "Well, I'm a grad student at LSU. Working with some of the professors there on their research, I came across some interesting stuff, especially about this house and Victoria Blanc."

"Like what?" Brian asked picking up his bishop.

"You know how Jayne didn't want to talk about how Victoria died? Well... suicide doesn't make sense."

"Why not? People kill themselves every day. I had an uncle who offed himself because he played the wrong lotto numbers," Marcus offered.

"Yeah, but there was no explanation. There was no note and the sharecroppers who worked the land before she died said that she was at odds with some of the local power brokers. And when her children returned, they found the house quite disturbed."

"How so?"

"The front door was busted in and there was blood on some of the walls, the stairs, and in her bedroom."

"Okay. You almost had me," Marcus chuckled. "Telling a creepy story like that in this house while we're in it during a storm like this... bravo! Let me guess... it was a guy with a hook that did it?"

"No. I'm serious. I read some of the correspondence between the children and they all had their suspicions."

"So... what happened?"

"I'm not sure. There were so many rumors about her life and the circumstances surrounding her death that it's hard to know what is true even in the archives. One thing I am sure about is that she didn't kill herself."

"What kind of rumors?" Marcus asked, playing with an ivory handled letter opener.

"For one thing, she was black."

"What does that have to do with anything?"

"She was white passing. One of the stories is that her husband knew about it after they exchanged vows. When he planned to annul the marriage, she hired Marie Laveau to do some voodoo on him. That's probably why he died so soon after they married. She got him out of the way before he could get rid of her."

Marcus laughed, thinking about finding a voodoo doctor to perform a spell on Lois.

"Because she controlled the plantation legally, she made the system of slavery work for her."

"What do you mean?" Brian asked

"She positioned the home to help enslaved people escape."

"Wait. I thought she was a slaveowner."

"In appearance," Calista said as she advanced another piece. "She actually kept black people on the property who wanted to stay. Slaves from other plantations would escape to this land to seek refuge. With this property being so close to New Orleans, they could easily hide among the free black population in the city, buy forged freedom papers, and leave from one of the ships at the port before anyone knew that they were gone."

Brian sat back in his chair. "Are you being real with us?"

"One hundred percent," Calista replied. "Now, the documents don't explicitly say who escaped through here, but there are interviews in the WPA slave narratives that talk about a white female plantation owner in the area smuggling slaves out of New Orleans."

"So, you think that is what got her killed?" Marcus asked.

"No. She didn't die until about 1879. By then, slavery had ended. Besides, no one suspected her of aiding the enslaved as she presented herself as a white plantation owner. The sheer amount of land and slaves she controlled never aroused anyone's suspicion."

"So, the slaves just hid on this plantation before heading to New Orleans?"

"Not just on this plantation... in this house."

"Bullshit," Marcus remarked. "They would have covered this on the tour."

"Not if they don't know about it."

15

Lucinda gingerly walked down the steps. Each board creaked under her feet as she descended. The flashlight from her phone brightly cast throughout the room. There was a faint dripping noise in the distance and a powerful aroma of mildew in the air that she struggled to block out.

Holding the phone above her head, Lucinda swept across the room searching for what secrets were being kept from the world. The dripping grew louder as she approached the source. As she looked to the ground, she discovered a small pool of liquid that had formed. Kneeling, Lucinda stretched her hand out to it. Running her fingers through the pool, she found it to be cold and sticky. As she rubbed her fingers together under the light, she saw the distinct rusty color of the substance on her skin.

Lucinda tilted her phone upward, searching for the source of the liquid. As she moved her hand, the light brightened the wall in front of her. She was met only with the dirt and stone that had formed the cellar she was exploring. Placing her hands on the stones, she found no dampness. Everything she ran her fingers over was dry to the touch. As she took a breath, she witnessed something move out of the corner of her eye on the wall.

"This   must   be   it." A trickle of liquid propelled down the wall in front of her. Perhaps rain had penetrated the foundation and found its way under the house. Lucinda placed her hand on the wall again. Everything was dry except for one spot. Out of curiosity, she poked her finger into the spot and began moving some of the loose dirt and material until she came to a stone facing an inch behind where she found the liquid on the wall. The sound of the drips continued behind her.

Lucinda pivoted, shining the light on the opposite wall. There was nothing other than more stone, dirt, and cobwebs. She returned to her investigation. Lucinda poked her index finger back into the wall contacting a small, smooth object. Feeling it loosen, she struggled to keep the light of the phone focused on the spot of her search. Lucinda freed the object, holding it in her palm.

With her hand open, she focused the light on her discovery. As she aimed the phone at the contents of her hand, she held her breath, befuddled at what she held. Lucinda lifted the object to her face, firmly held between her thumb and index finger. It was unmistakable despite the grit and dirt surrounding it. Her skin crawled

at the realization of holding the molar between her fingers.

Shocked, Lucinda lost her grip of the tooth, dropping it to the ground. Its impact on the ground was marked by a dull thud. She knelt, searching for it knowing that she had to let the others know what she found. Lucinda looked at the ground and was introduced to a ghastly sight. Teeth were scattered in front of her on the ground. Lucinda's breath arrested. She could hear her heartbeat. It was the only sign for her that confirmed she was not in a dream. She was disoriented, uncertain of what she had discovered and unsure of what to do in this moment.

"*Help me*," a faint cry from the darkness whispered.

Lucinda didn't know where the voice had come from. She didn't know what to make of it. She didn't know what direction was safe for her to head.

"*Help me*," the voice called out again.

Lucinda nervously walked away from the voice, aiming the light into the darkness. Her phone signaled a low battery warning.

"Not now," she pleaded.

As she looked up from her phone, she found herself staring into a strange figure with a dark face. Lucinda's reaction was muted. She tried to speak, but her mouth would not comply. She tried to move and found her body was unwilling. The man's face was hardened and scarred. Lucinda looked into his eyes as he uttered the words "*help me*" once more. She did not know what to do. She did not know how she could comfort the man. Her safety had taken a backseat to this man's concern. Lucinda reached out her hand to touch him.

"*Help me*," he pleaded. "*I'm going to die down here.*"
Blood poured from his eyes and his mouth with each word he spoke.

"I... I can't," Lucinda replied.

She stepped away from the figure as he continued to plead with her.

"*Quiet. I can hear them coming*," he pointed his gnarled finger behind Lucinda.

She turned her head, looking in the direction he pointed.

"I don't hear anyone... I don't see anything," she said as she peered over her shoulder.

Lucinda turned back to the man, finding him gone. All that remained where he stood were teeth and blood–stained earth.

Lucinda retraced her steps in the corridor. Seeing a sliver of light, she pushed against the surface, finding herself back in the library where Marcus, Brian, and Calista were engaged in conversation.

Noticing his disheartened friend, Marcus asked "What the hell happened to you?"

Not knowing how to explain and not fully comprehending what took place, Lucinda did not respond. She quietly sat down behind the desk and thought about what she came across. She looked out the window. The storm still raged outside. Lucinda wanted to leave but knew that there would be no escape from the house that night.

16

Donna overheard the commotion in the next room. She looked through the doorway seeing Margaret and Trudy engaged in a frantic discussion.

"*Psst*," she called over to Lois, Daphne, and Dolores.

"What is it?" Lois asked, annoyed.

"I don't know... but come check it out," she motioned to her friends.

Dolores and Daphne stacked themselves against the door opening as they listened in. Their faces quickly took a grim turn as they realized the severity of what was being discussed.

"Did they say the tour guide is dead?" Daphne asked.

"Bullshit!" Dolores responded in shock.

"That's what I heard!" Daphne whispered forcefully. "They said something about a gun."

"Someone brought a gun?" Donna asked.

"Great. We found ourselves on a murder tour. Everyone told me that I would get killed if I went to New Orleans." Lois groaned.

The four of them were flustered as they considered what had been overheard.

"We need to find Brian and his sister," Daphne offered.

"How are we going to get past them?" Dolores asked.

"I don't know... just look around for something we can use to protect ourselves."

The group scoured the kitchen, searching the drawers and cabinets finding nothing more than vacant shelves. Donna, reaching into her bag, pulled out a bejeweled object.

"I still have my mace," she said, holding up the can.

The four of them gave her a small sign of approval and gathered behind her as they exited the kitchen, heading into the dining room.

Donna held the mace at her hip as she prepared to quickly draw it, if needed. She wanted to be ready but wanted to remain inconspicuous. The four women walked carefully through the dining room as they planned to reconnect with Brian, Lucinda, and Marcus. Their eyes focused on Margaret and Trudy as they continued their conversation. Margaret's eyes were red and weary. The group grasped a different tone as they sensed their misjudgment of the events leading to their entry into the room.

"Is everything alright?" Lois asked.

"She's just a little upset about Jayne," Trudy responded.

"What happened?" Donna asked, tightening her grip on the can of mace.

Trudy, rubbing her friend's shoulders, caught the others up on the night's events informing them about a prank that had gone awry and resulted in the sudden and violent death of their tour guide. She tried to spare them the gory details as much as she could as not to traumatize Margaret any further.

Lois, Donna, Dolores, and Daphne all took a deep breath as their fears were assuaged. They turned their attention to their previous purpose in finding Brian in the library. The four of them continued through the room approaching the foyer. Despite being reassured with the removal of danger from their fellow tour members, they were still on edge. The women conversed about the events that had just been explained to them. Huddling together, they crusaded forward.

As they crossed the threshold, the lightning outside flashed, illuminating the room. Donna and Daphne were startled as the light unsettled them. Shadows appeared on the walls and danced around them. The women huddled closer and held on to each other as they trekked along.

Entering the grand foyer, a figure rounded the corner. Donna, panicking, quickly raised the small can of mace. Nervously, she screamed and pressed the trigger, releasing the contents into her own face. The mist contacted her eyes, nose, and mouth. Her friends turned their heads in time, avoiding much of the blast. Donna, blinded, stumbled into Dolores. Daphne coughed repeatedly. Lois fell to her knees. Dolores, knocked over by Donna, ran into the wall.

Eli and Eric approached the coughing spectacle and helped the women to their feet. Margaret and Trudy approached the scattered chaos, confused, shocked, and a little amused.

As the others approached, the mace entered their nostrils and constricted their breathing. Their eyes were impacted by the residue, blurring their vision. Trudy and Margaret grabbed Lois and Daphne, guiding them to the kitchen sink to rinse their eyes and provide them with some relief.

Eli grabbed Dolores from the floor, taking her into the bathroom. Hearing the disturbance outside of the library, Marcus and Brian emerged, quickly assisting the women as Lucinda and Calista followed behind.

They were all quickly caught off guard by the spray lingering in the air. Their eyes watered and their skin became itchy. Marcus began coughing and sneezing as his body reacted to the irritant in the air. Donna fought off help as she was overcome by the pain in her eyes and the burning of her skin. Brian, grabbing her, noticed that her eyes were swollen and red. He looked outside to see the rain still heavily falling. Brian knew that the constant cooling rain would help alleviate the burning in her eyes.

He grabbed the doorknob. It did not budge. Donna's groans and expressions of pain continued. Brian calmly grabbed her, walking Donna into the kitchen where he found a crowd around the sink. The party each took turns rinsing their faces with the cold water available to rid themselves of the burning sensation. As their condition subsided, they all returned to the dining room. Their eyes stung and their skin remained irritated, but nothing compared to the intensity they had all experienced initially.

Sitting at the table, Brian and Marcus were brought up to speed as to the events surrounding Jayne's demise. Brian seemed dismayed at the thought of what had happened and the circumstances involving it.

"What can we do?" Margaret asked.

"Well, nothing. You already tried calling the police. Does anyone else have a signal?" Brian asked.

Everyone checked their phones, quickly learning that there was no service available.

"Well, all we really can do is continue waiting here until we get a signal or if the driver happens to show up," Brian stated.

"Wait, what about Jayne's phone?" Lucinda asked. "Hers might have a signal. We could try the police again, plus her phone has the number for the driver."

"Good thinking," Brian said. "I'll go up and check. Anyone want to help?"

Thinking about Jayne's corpse unsettled Brian. He had only seen a few dead bodies, mostly at funerals. The only other time was when he had to work with a cadaver during pre-med. Marcus sensed the disturbance in his friend. Approaching, Brian, he patted his shoulder.

"Come on man," he said, reassuring him.

Grabbing one of the lanterns, the two walked up the stairs. They prepared themselves for what possible macabre scene awaited them. Margaret rung her hands as she watched them ascend from the threshold of the dining room. Lucinda, still processing her experiences in the cellar, stared out the window. The others trying to occupy their minds, waited for Brian and Marcus to return.

Arriving at the landing, Marcus stepped in front of Brian, placing his hand on the doorknob.

"I've always wanted to do this."

"What?" Brian asked, confused.

A big grin formed on Marcus' face.

"Wanna see a dead body?"

Brian rolled his eyes at his friend's attempt at dark humor. He knew that this was neither the place nor the time, but he had grown accustomed to Marcus making outlandish or inappropriate jokes to help break the tension or to mask his own insecurities.

Marcus turned the knob. Swinging the door open, they saw Jayne's lifeless, distorted body on the floor. It was even more grotesque than described downstairs. Jayne's body lay upon a large rug on the floor.

Brian knelt next to Jayne's body. Brian grabbed a corner of the blood–soaked rug, pulling it over Jayne's disfigured head. Rolling the corpse on its side, Brian and Marcus searched through Jayne's pockets. Finding her phone, Marcus pressed Jayne's thumb onto the screen, unlocking it. Despite the discovery, the two were dismayed as her phone displayed no service as available.

"What a waste," Marcus sighed.

"Maybe not," Brian stated, his attention drawn to several dark spots on the wood floorboards that were previously hidden by the rug. Even in the darkened room, the blemishes were noticeable.

"You see this?" Brian asked, pointing to the discolorations.

"Spots? What of it?" he asked.

"Yeah. They look like blood stains."

"From Jayne?"

"No. These are too old and judging from where her body is, she couldn't have bled over here."

"Ok. So? It's old blood. I'm sure there is a lot of old stuff in this house."

"Yeah. But you remember what Calista was telling us downstairs about her suspicions?" Brian asked.

"Yeah."

"Hey. Call her up here."

Marcus exited the room, approaching the landing. He called down asking for Calista to join them in the main bedroom. After being reassured that Jayne was not visible, she joined Marcus and Brian.

Calista kept her head down as she entered the room, hoping not to catch a glimpse of the corpse. Brian motioned to where he was kneeling.

"I think you may have been on to

something," he said, pointing to the blood splotches. As he rose, his weight dislodged one of the floorboards.

Calista looked down at the blood–stained boards, questioning their cause. Her inquiry into them came to an end as she found herself distracted by what lay under the raised flooring.

Kneeling next to the board, Calista placed her fingers in the spacing, loosening the grip the board had with the framing. With the board removed, she investigated the vacant space of the flooring. She looked up at Marcus and Brian with a smile stretching the width of her face.

17

The group grew anxious as they waited for Marcus, Brian, and Calista to return. Rain continued pounding the building. The rapping on the windows made them even more restless. Sweat trickled down Margaret's back.

"It's too warm in here. I need some air," she said fanning herself with her hands.

"Are you okay?" Trudy asked.

Sweat poured down Margaret's face. She furiously wiped the perspiration from her brow.

"I... I just can't catch my breath," she replied.

Trudy walked over to her friend imploring her to sit. Margaret brushed off her concerns.

"I just need some air."

Margaret tried opening a window, but it

would not budge. She tried another and was met with the same result. Frustrated, she walked to the entrance. She grabbed the knob. It would not turn. More perspiration fell.

"I need some air."

Reaching out, Trudy attempted to soothe Margaret's discomfort. Margaret continued her attempts to open the door. She was frantic.

"Margaret, it's going to be okay."

"I need some air," she said with stifled breath, pushing Trudy away.

Margaret grabbed the doorknob once more and was met with a tremendous shock. Her body was lifted several feet off the ground. Speechless, she remained suspended in the air. Trudy covered her mouth with both of her hands. She watched as Margaret's body rapidly propelled toward the entrance.

Impacting a crossbeam over the entrance, Margaret's face was split open. Her blood rained down to the floor. She was thrown backward before being thrust into the wall again. Her head impacted the wall repeatedly before her body dropped to the floor.

The others watched in horror as Margaret was tossed around the room like a toy thrown by an angry child. A gurgle emerged from her throat as she took her final breaths. Trudy ran over to her friend's body, kneeling next to her.

Margaret lie face down on the floor. There was no light in her eyes. Her body was motionless.

"What the *fuck* is happening here?" Trudy screamed. She knew now that her earlier encounter had not been the result of her imagination. Something was in this house. Watching her friend die confirmed it for her. She remained unsure of what to make of what had happened. The others looked on in shock not knowing what to do and not knowing what they had just witnessed. Blood pooled around Margaret's body. Trudy rose, stepping away from Margaret as the blood approached her feet.

Lucinda looked around at the others as they processed the events. Some wringing their hands, others turning their heads away.

"What did we get ourselves into?" she asked herself.

18

Calista's eyes focused on a small wooden chest in the flooring. Opening the trunk, she discovered a large leather-bound book laying among papers, pictures, and other items. Picking up the book, she brushed the cover with her fingers, freeing its dust and debris. She slowly turned the pages, reading the entries.

"What is it?" Marcus asked as he knelt to her level.

"I'm not sure, but it looks like a diary or journal," she replied.

"Okay, but why would it be hidden in the floorboard?" Brian asked.

Calista flipped through the pages as she attempted to gain a greater understanding of the book and its contents. The book revealed Victoria Blanc's personal thoughts on matters of politics, the truth about her children, the home and land, and the local community. Calista continued to read as Marcus and Brian looked on, hoping for her to inform them about the contents.

"Oh my God," she blurted.

"What? What is it?" Brian asked.

"Just holding this. I never imagined that I would ever find anything close to supporting what I had been researching... but this has exceeded any of my expectations. This book is a wealth of knowledge and a missing link to explaining so much... I just can't put into words what this book means not just to me, but to telling an accurate representation of the history of this area and beyond." Her faced flushed as she continued flipping through the pages.

"Okay, but what does it say?" Marcus asked.

"Everything. There are personal letters wedged between some of the pages. Look at this," she said as she pulled out a document. "This is a freedom petition. They were used by enslaved people or those sponsoring them to request their emancipation through the courts."

Marcus gave a blank look hearing the information. Noticing his confusion about the meaning of the document, Calista elaborated.

"It worked a bit like this, there were

very few options for enslaved people to become emancipated. If someone had a valid reason to become free, they had to file a case with the court. Say you were never enslaved, and someone walked up to you on the street in New Orleans trying to claim you as theirs. You've never been enslaved so you don't have papers to prove that you aren't a slave. If you are lucky, someone from your community finds out about your abduction and notifies the police. They then take you into custody and house you in the city jail. A petition is filed on your behalf and the judge determines whether or not you are free. If the case goes your way, the court has an official judgment that lists you as free and you are then backed up by a legal document. The judgment is published in the local newspapers notifying everyone that you are free. Another way is that you are such a 'good and loyal slave...' I almost threw up saying those words, but I digress. If you earn the favor of your slaveholder and he or she has no more use for you, they file a petition with the court requesting for you to be recognized as free."

"Sounds like a good deal," Brian replied.

"Yeah, if you can get the system to work for you, you have no issues aside from the racism that you may encounter daily. Besides, it was much more common for women to be freed through this process than for men, especially after some of the slave revolts."

"Why is that?" Brian asked.

"Free Black men were seen as a threat, especially if there were too many of them. It was believed that Black men were constantly plotting to overthrow slave owners."

"No, I mean, why is it that women were freed more often than men?"

"Let me put it this way, would you want the mother of your child to be considered a slave when she gave birth to your children?"

"Come again?" Marcus responded.

"Slave owners raped and impregnated their enslaved workers and would often free them prior to giving birth so their wives could not sell the children. The option that these men had was to free these women through the courts so they could not be claimed as property. If the women are freed before they have their children, the children are recognized as free. Many of them would settle in the black neighborhoods of New Orleans and remain in contact with their former owners who served as their benefactors paying for their housing, children's educations, and businesses."

"Holy shit," Marcus blurted, astonished. Calista smirked, acknowledging the remarkable nature of the arrangement. She continued reading through the book, stopping occasionally as she came to information that caught her attention.

"Maybe we should head back downstairs?" Brian asked as his attention returned to Jayne's body.

"One moment," Calista responded, pulling the text closer to her face.

"Find something else interesting?" Marcus asked.

"Maybe, but it doesn't make sense. There's probably better light downstairs," she said, closing the book. "Let's go," she told Marcus and Brian.

The three exited the room quietly. Brian glanced back at the body, reflecting on the turn his evening had taken. As they approached the landing, Brian stopped. His eyes focused on the wall across from where they stood.

"Something isn't right here," Brian said.

"No kidding. We just covered up a dead body in an old plantation house," Marcus responded.

"No... not that. Is something missing? I mean... wasn't there a portrait inside of that frame earlier?"

Calista and Marcus strained their eyes looking in the direction of Brian's attention.

"I mean, I see the frame, but nothing else," Brian stated.

The gilded frame posted over the stairs held a vacant print. The home of Victoria Blanc's imposing likeness had departed. Where she was once perched on the wall with her beloved cat, Bishop, the trio found a void. Brian thought that it may have been the dimly lit area and fatigue preventing him from seeing the image. He held up the lantern, placing his hand against the frame. He moved his hand closer to feel the canvas. Touching the painting gave Brian relief as he could feel the brush strokes, but he despaired as there was no image to match the patterns his hand felt.

"It's gone," Brian informed the others.

Marcus and Calista stepped forward to see if Brian was overlooking the image. They questioned to themselves if the painting had existed in this spot. They were certain, but at this moment, they were unsure of what, if anything, occupied this spot.

"No idea, man. I really don't remember the painting. I remember Jayne saying something about it, but I wasn't paying attention," Marcus stated, scratching his head.

Marcus sighed and continued downstairs, passing in front of Brian. He closely watched his steps as he descended, holding on to the railing. With the low light of the room, he did not want to risk adding falling down a flight of stairs to the evening. He approached the bottom of the stairs with Brian and Calista following closely.

Stepping forward, Marcus' foot met an obstacle on the floor causing his body to tumble forward. He landed face down, the impact of his body on the wooden floor casting a light rumble through the threshold. The sound startled Anne who had been consoling Trudy in the dining room. Donna, Dolores, Daphne, and Lois turned to see Marcus on the floor after briefly thinking that Margaret's body had ascended and impacted the walls again.

"Oh, it's just you," Donna remarked.

"That's quite a warm greeting," Marcus chuckled lowly, dusting himself off. Marcus scanned the room trying to recall everyone who had been in the room prior to his and Brian's departure upstairs. He turned to see Brian still on the outside of the room standing in silence with Calista.

"I'm good, man," Marcus said as he held his thumb up.

"It's not that, Marcus. Look down," Brian responded.

Marcus turned his gaze downward. As he focused, he saw a body lying on the floor. He stepped closer, seeing there was no movement... no sign of life.

"Oh, fuck! What the hell happened down here?" he asked, raising his voice.

"We don't know," Anne responded, fighting

back tears. "She just got thrown around the room. It was horrible. We could hear her bones breaking. I've never seen anything like that. It was horrible."

"Thrown around?" Brian asked, puzzled. "Is everyone else okay?"

"As good as we can be," Eric stated.

Everyone else sat around the table in shock. They could not comprehend or process what they had witnessed, nor did they want to. The joy and intrigue they found in the tour had long departed. They found themselves questioning what fate awaited them. They feared that they may never leave.

Eric's frustration mounted. He seethed. The rain, thunder, and lightning outside goaded him. The flickering of the candles in the house elevated his anxiety. He looked across the room at Margaret's body. He stared at her, contemplating what he should do.

The guilt of Jayne's death hung over him. He did not express anything to the others but felt as though everything that happened this night was his fault. He didn't know what to do. He didn't know how to make things right. He just knew that he needed to leave. He didn't need to be around anyone else. Being in that house, he felt, would result in further harm to everyone there.

He tried to get Margaret and Jayne out of his thoughts as he turned and faced the window. The crashing of the thunder and the flashing of the lightning did little to distract his mind. He heard a faint whisper in his ear.

"*You don't belong here...*" the voice called. He looked around seeing that no one from the group was close to him at the table.

"*You don't belong here...*" the voice whispered again.

Eric stood from the table, wringing his hands. The voice resonated in his mind. He did not feel safe. He needed to find a way out of the house. He walked to the kitchen. He buried his head on the preparation table hoping something would drown out his thoughts and the voice that had entered his mind. He wanted to escape. More importantly, he needed to get out of this house. Raising his head, he saw the side door leading outside to the porch.

He gently grabbed the doorknob. Turning it, the door opened allowing a cool rush of air into the kitchen. The air and mist on his face was refreshing. He stepped out onto the porch. As he took a deep breath, the door slammed behind him. Startled, he turned to grab the doorknob and attempt reentry into the building. As he struggled with the doorknob, he heard faint laughter behind him and saw a woman's smile through the glass of the adjacent window. He pounded on the door. No one responded.

He yelled for the others to open the door. He thought to himself about what a horrible time for someone to attempt a prank on him or to even joke around. He walked around the porch peering into the windows, hoping to gain someone's attention. Eric saw the others in the dining room. He called to them, knocking on the windows. They did not look up. He raised his voice, but each time it was drowned out by the thunder.

"Fuck this," he said to himself.

Eric walked to the front of the building before proceeding around to the other side of the house. He hoped to find another door or window that was open or unlocked so he could reenter. The rain blew sideways, drenching him. The precipitation washed over his body with each step. He attempted to open each window he came across. Nothing would allow him access. Each window was locked, and each door failed to open. He continued until he found himself where he started outside of the kitchen. The door was slightly ajar.

He stepped forward, crossing into the room. As his left foot hit the floor, he felt a sharp pain in his right heel. He tried to put weight on it, and the pain increased. Losing his balance, he fell to the ground. The pain was unbearable. There w as a searing p ain r adiating u p h is l eg. Eric winced as he rotated his foot attempting to soothe the pain. It only made the sensation worse. Sliding his sock down, he discovered his Achilles tendon had been severed. Blood trickled onto the floor. Eric's confusion rivaled the physical pain he felt in his leg. He called out for help. Confused, Daphne and Donna entered the room.

Seeing the blood on the floor and Eric holding his leg, they rushed over. They each grabbed a towel from the counter and applied pressure to his leg.

"Can you stand?" Donna asked.

"I think I can, now," he responded.

"Good. Well let's get you over to the table and sit you down," Daphne added. "What happened?"

"I don't know. I went outside and got locked out. When I came back in, I fell to the ground and saw my leg was bleeding."

Donna and Daphne lifted Eric to his feet. As he ascended, he was pulled away from the women. Eric stood upright; his arms outstretched forcefully. His body was turned with his back facing the women.

They screamed as they watched as his shirt was torn open, exposing his bare back. They heard a woman's laughter as his skin was split open. With each slash of his skin, they could hear the crack of a whip and the tearing of his flesh.

Daphne and Donna's screaming alerted the others in the dining room who quickly rushed to meet them. They were introduced to the horror of hearing Eric's screams as he was methodically tortured in front of them.

Blood poured from the wounds on his back. Eli ran forward to grab his friend and was immediately repelled and thrown into the wall. His head impacted the window framing, cutting his jaw. Concussed, he struggled to get to his feet. Anne checked on him as the others tried to help Eric. They could not get close to him and were helpless as they watched strips of flesh torn away from his skin in a checkered pattern.

Eric's screams faded as he collapsed to the floor. His shirt was soaked in blood. Brian approached him, checking his breathing and pulse. Neither was present. Eric's body went cold on the kitchen floor. His eyes blankly stared at the wall. Brian placed his hands over Eric's eyes, closing them.

Marcus let out a deep breath, hands behind his neck, asking, "What is going on in this house?"

Calista held the journal tight to her chest. She had not taken a breath until Marcus spoke. Daphne and Donna held each other, crying. Lois fell to her knees on the floor. Lucinda shook her head in disbelief.

"Something is wrong with this house. I thought it was just my mind playing tricks on me, but I found something in the cellar."

"What are you talking about?" Brian asked, his eyes still fixed on Eric's body.

"When we were in the library, I found a door that led to a cellar. There was something down there. I don't know how to explain it. But it asked for my help. I thought I was imagining it. When I came back, you guys were still playing chess and I thought that it must have been in my head."

"What did you see?" Marcus asked.

"It was a man. His face was scarred. He looked like he had been tortured."

"Who? What was it?"

"It was a man, I think. He asked for my help and that he was dying. Then he disappeared," she stated.

"Disappeared?" Lois asked. "What are we in a haunted house?"

"How else do you explain what has been happening?" Anne asked.

"Haunted houses aren't real. Ghosts aren't real. This is bullshit. There has to be another explanation for all of this," Lois shot back.

"Look, I don't know about you, but I've

never seen a person suspended in the air and have random slashes form on their body. Something is happening here. I don't want to debate what anyone believes in or doesn't believe in. I know what I saw, and I am not staying here any longer. I don't care if I have to hotwire that bus or swim out of here, I am getting away from this house," Trudy stated. "You all can stay here; I'm leaving before anything else happens."

19

Trudy stepped past the group, avoiding looking at Eric's body. She ignored her pulse as it began to rise. She focused her breathing while moving toward the door connecting the kitchen and the porch.

"Stay here. We need to figure out what is going on," Brian called out to her.

"No. I'm not going to die here. Anyone who wants to come with me, I'll be in the bus," she replied.

The group glanced at each other looking for a sign or agreement of what to do. Trudy walked out of the door as the others watched her exit.

Calista held the book tighter to her chest.

Without blinking, without flinching, Calista whispered, "We can't leave."

As the words exited her mouth, the door violently closed behind Trudy. The sound startled the group. They watched Trudy through the windows as she made her way around the house. They followed behind her in the dining room looking out the windows as she continued her trek. With faces pressed against the glass, they watched the storm continue outside. The trees continued swaying from the strong winds. The lightning lit up the night's sky. The thunder boomed its disapproval.

Trudy stopped at the top of the entrance stairs, gauging the distance to the bus. She saw the water moving the loose dirt in front of the building as she carefully planned her voyage. Trudy did not want to misstep, finding herself stuck in the mud.

The others anxiously watched as Trudy took her first step off the porch. The lightning struck, startling them. She took another step and was met with the boom of thunder.

Consumed with her mission, Trudy descended from the final step and into the mud. The muck and grime enveloped her foot. Undeterred, she took another step forward. Her other foot was consumed by the ground. The damp earth reached her ankles as she sank sharply into the ground. The others watched as she trudged toward the bus. They remained calm as the distance between Trudy and the bus became shorter.

With each step she made, the group inside grew more confident that they would get off the property. Hours earlier, their concerns were about missing their flights, or not getting enough sleep. Now, they were held captive. Their safety and their lives were endangered.

Trudy chuckled to herself about the absurdity of the walk. Her feet sloshed through the muck. Her shoes became heavier with each step. The downpour of rain increased, continuing to surround her. Wiping the rain from her eyes, she could estimate she had ten to fifteen more steps before arriving at the vehicle. She stepped forward. She took another step followed by another before feeling her foot being sucked into the ground. She pulled at her leg trying to free herself. With a strong tug she freed herself, losing her shoe in the process.

Turning to retrieve her shoe, she found her other foot stuck. Pulling her foot free, she lost her second shoe. Trudy, disturbed by the sensation of the mud on her socks, found herself distracted from her primary purpose in reaching the bus. She was now overcome with retrieving her shoes before continuing her voyage.

Kneeling in the mud, she attempted to dig out her shoes. A seal bound her first shoe to the ground as she pulled at it. With two firm tugs, she dislodged it. She looked to the ground for her other shoe. Finding the hole, she reached into the ground. Trudy pulled at her shoe. She struggled to dislodge it. She reached deeper, hoping to gain a better grasp on her shoe. She pulled her hand out, empty. Reaching in again, she grabbed on to the shoe more forcefully. Trudy's grip on the shoe made her certain that she would regain it.

As she pulled, the mud rose up her arm, wrapping around her elbow. She continued to pull and found herself deeper into the mud. She pulled harder, her chest now inches from the surface. Undeterred, she did not want to lose this battle with the earth. Pushing against the ground with her other arm, she could not break free. The grip of the mud grew tighter. It covered both of her arms, her legs, and torso, before reaching the base of her neck. Trudy looked at the mud and her eyes widened. Arms had emerged from the ground, pulling her into the earth. She screamed. A hand tightly wrapped around her mouth. The rain increased in intensity blurring the vision of those watching from the house.

Trudy's chest tightened as the arms wrapped around her, constricting her breathing.

She could not call for help. She could not signal to the others as to the danger she faced. She winced and wept as her mouth remained covered by the hand. Her muscles tightened and fatigued as she resisted being pulled into the ground. She struggled to breathe.

Dragging her into the muck, the arms tightened their grip. Her head slowly sank into the mud. Sinking, her eyes caught a glimpse of the building where the others watched as she was consumed by the earth. Her mouth filled with water and mud as she gasped for air and struggled against the force pulling her down.

Trudy's fight was a lost cause as she sunk deeper into the earth, the air in her lungs being replaced by water and debris. Her struggle ceased as one last pocket of air escaped her body.

20

"What's going on out there? Did she make it?" Anne asked.

The sheets of rain blurred their vision of the scene. The group lost sight of Trudy as her distance from the porch grew. They waited in anticipation for the bus to approach. Minutes passed and there was nothing to reassure them that she had been successful.

Eli stepped past the group, walking to the foyer.

"We have to do something," he said with mild confidence.

Eli walked over to Margaret's body that lay in front of the door. Grabbing her feet, he pulled her away from the entrance, leaving a trail of blood on the floor. Dropping her legs, he returned to the entrance. He grabbed the knob, slowly turning it. A low click sounded, ensuring the door was a viable option for him to escape the madness that the night had brought. He looked back at the others as they quietly watched him exit the building. The door swayed slowly back and forth connecting the outside world with the horrors held within the house. Eli reached the top of the stairs as he proceeded to pursue Trudy and arrive at the bus.

Gingerly, he descended the stairs and found himself ankle deep in the mud. Momentarily, he was disturbed at the sensation in his shoes as the cold, damp earth wrapped around his feet. Eli slogged a few steps through the mud following the same path that Trudy had paved. He continued forward, finding a short distance between himself and the bus. As he continued, he felt a tug at his right foot. The grip tightened, preventing him from moving forward. Eli looked to the ground, trying to discover the obstacle that prevented him from continuing. Reaching down, he tried freeing himself. His hand searched below the surface of the water and mud finding an object gripping the top of his foot. Eli questioned the identity of what held him in place.

He grabbed the firm, slender object.

"Tree roots," he scoffed as he looked around,

examining his surroundings.

Eli yanked at the root, loosening the hold it had on him. He pulled more, bringing the root above the surface. Relieved, he pulled his foot out of the space that it had once occupied. His comfort was quickly broken as he looked down to see a hand reaching out from the ground. His heart jumped, causing him to forget his purpose outside.

Eli rushed back to the house. The others watched through the open door as he struggled to run in the mud. Losing his balance, he fell forward into a shallow puddle. Eli picked himself up and frantically continued toward the stairs.

He stumbled again, finding himself at the base of the building. Placing one hand on the banister, Eli lifted himself from the ground. As he stood, he felt his neck tightening. Eli grabbed at his throat trying to seek relief. The others could not determine his state. They did not understand what danger he faced. Eli's body rose from the ground.

The group watched as his feet draped then dangled. He could not speak. He could not call out for help. The others did not know what to do. All they could do was watch as his slow ascent continued. His upward motion ceasing, Eli hung in the air with his legs kicking wildly. His hands were tugging at something around his neck. He felt the pressure grow. As he hung in the air, he looked to the group watching at the door, paralyzed.

He reached out one of his hands from his neck to them. Anne called out to him. As she stepped forward, his body sharply dropped and hung in place a few feet from the ground. His neck bent. His eyes widened. His arms held limply at his sides. Several of the members of the tour screamed. The lightning flashed and his cold body landed in the mud. The thunder rumbled as the terror sunk in for the others.

Marcus slowly closed the door in disbelief. Brian and Lucinda sat on the stairs. Anne stood at the door, staring into the wood surface. Lois, Donna, Dolores, and Daphne walked to the dining table together processing what they just witnessed. Calista held the book open under the nearest candle and returned to reading the text.

Brian, noticing Calista's face buried in the text, overlooked her decision as simply her way of dealing with the shock of what happened. Lucinda placed her hands on her knees. Taking a deep breath, she scratched her head. As she exhaled, she knew the gravity of what she experienced earlier needed to be addressed.

"Everyone. I don't know how to put this, so I am just going to say it," Lucinda stated. "Unless we figure out what is going on here, we are all going to die tonight."

Lois, frustrated, responded, "How exactly are we going to do that? We can't Google how to get out of a haunted house."

Lucinda rose to her feet and walked over to Lois who was slouched over the table.

"This was your idea to come here. For some reason, you thought visiting this place would be a good idea. To be honest, I don't give two shits about you, but my brother... my brother over there is all that matters to me tonight. I want to get the fuck out of here alive. I want him to get out of here alive. If the house or whatever is in this house wants to keep you here, I won't lose any sleep over it."

"Guys, stop!" Brian stepped between his sister and his fiancée. "Now's not the time for us to point fingers or blame anyone. We need to figure out how to get out of here!"

Lois and Lucinda glared at each other, waiting for the other to move.

"Sit down... both of you. Calm down," Brian demanded.

"Calm? How the hell do you suppose we remain calm?" Daphne asked.

Brian ignored her remark and approached Calista. She looked up from the book to see him standing inches away from her.

"You seem to know a lot about this house

and the history of it. What do you think?"

"I... I don't know. I thought I knew a lot, but this book broke me of that certainty."

"What do you mean?" he asked.

"This book has years of reflections and information written in Victoria Blanc's hand. There is stuff in here about her trips to New Orleans, getting black people to vote, and the threats that were made to her life for doing so many things that didn't meet with the approval of the white population here."

"So, nothing about the house having something like this happen when she was alive?"

"Nothing. The only thing that comes even close is the last entry," Calista said flipping the book open to the last filled page. "Look. She writes about how a group of men were coming to her home and how she wouldn't see the next sunrise. And right here," she said, pointing to one line in the book, "she states that if her blood were shed on the land, she would return to terrorize those who violated her legacy. And right here," she read the line, "'The history of this home will haunt all those who enter. The more they deny it, the stronger the terror will grow.' Nothing about what to do to avoid it. If, like I think, she was murdered on these grounds, then there is no escape. We have to face what is here."

"Then why is it coming after all of us?"

Anne asked.

"It's like Jayne said when we came back into the house, the descendants expressly forbid anyone from staying overnight in this home," Calista answered.

Marcus, leaning against the wall responded, "If we are the first ones to stay here overnight, then she has been waiting a long time."

"Yeah... roughly one hundred and forty years," Calista said.

"What does this have to do with us? Why us? What did we do? What did the others do? Why is this happening?" Anne asked.

"Fuck why it's happening; we are way past that. I want to know how we get out of here. I don't like being held at the whim of a dead woman," Lois said, sharply.

"Okay. It's obvious what we need to do: make it until the morning. We don't do anything to the house. We don't try to leave. It only makes sense since the only restriction seemed that we aren't supposed to be here at night," Brian offered.

"I was worried you were going to say that," Marcus said.

"We've got no choice," Lucinda added.

21

Brian checked his watch.

3:18

"Okay. The sun should be up around six. We just need to keep our wits and sit still in this house," he stated.

The group sat in silence as they blocked all thoughts of their dead friends and acquaintances. The beating of the raindrops drowned out their thoughts. The flickering of the candles distracted them momentarily from the despair they felt. Anne sat alone on the floor, the lone member of her team who remained. Brian, Marcus, and Lucinda sat by the window, willing the sun to rise, putting an end to this nightmare. Daphne, Donna, Dolores, and Lois repeatedly checked their phones. Calista held the book under a candle at the table, hoping to find some bit of information that could help.

Frustrated, Daphne rose. Walking from the dining room, into the kitchen, from the kitchen to the music room, she searched for a signal on her phone. As she moved around the house, her hopes of finding any connection with the outside world were quickly dashed. Discouraged, she placed the phone back into her pocket. As she turned, she felt she was being watched. Daphne stopped.

Looking around the room, she saw a small, dark figure on the floor. She waited, hoping that it was just her imagination. Her anxiety was confirmed as the figured moved. Her curiosity prompted her to step closer to the figure. It moved again. Daphne inched her way forward. The figure did not move. Its silhouette took a more defined form. She leaned forward to get a better glimpse. The figure moved away before stopping again. Daphne followed.

Keeping her eyes trained on the figure, she cautiously followed as it exited the room. The figure paused once more before Daphne's ears picked up the distinct sound of a low growl. Startled, she stood in silence. The figure approached her. Daphne's discomfort relaxed as the figure expressed a sharp mew in her direction.

"Jesus Christ, kitty," she chortled.

Daphne knelt to pet the animal. It withdrew as she extended her hand. The cat walked into the corridor. Looking over its shoulder, it waited for Daphne. She followed the cat as it passed through a doorway. Daphne copied its path, entering the small powder room under the stairway. Daphne shut the door behind her, preventing the escape of her new friend. She looked to the floor; the cat was nowhere to be found.

Taking her phone out of her pocket, she turned the screen on, subtly illuminating the room. She looked under the basin. She looked on the shelving. She moved the phone in her hand throughout the small room, finding nothing. Daphne caught a reflection of herself in the mirror. The fatigue was clear. The stress of the night had worn her face. Turning on the faucet, she wanted to refresh herself. She placed the phone on the edge of the sink to free her hands, allowing her to splash the water onto her face.

The cool water relieved some of the tension. She tilted her head back, letting out a heavy sigh before yawning. Placing her hands on the faucet, she turned off the water. Her phone screen lit up brighter as it vibrated, alerting her to a message. Looking down, she saw a new notification and one bar of signal strength. Excited, she picked up her phone. The light bounced off the mirror.

Calling her voicemail, Daphne looked into the mirror. She could only hear static in the message. The excitement at having some connection outside of this house diminished as the call ended. Holding up her phone, the bars had disappeared. Sullen, she placed her phone down. She held the sides of the sink as she stared at her reflection. The small amount of light distorted her image in the reflection. She stood there looking at herself. A small knock behind her broke Daphne's focus. She turned back seeing nothing behind herself.

Disillusioned, she turned back to the mirror, finding herself staring at a woman who smiled back at her. The woman reached out to Daphne as she was frozen in place at the sight of her. The woman grabbed her arms and held them down on the edges of the sink.

The woman laughed as Daphne struggled against her grip. She could not break free. The hands on her wrists tightened. The woman would not release her. The woman's smile grew. Daphne stared into the woman's eyes as her grin widened. The woman fixed her dark, ominous eyes on Daphne as she struggled. Her laugh terrified Daphne. Overcome with fright, she screamed. The woman laughed even more, releasing her grip.

Daphne lost her balance, falling into the wall behind her. She regained her composure and returned to the sink. She was convinced that she was imagining what took place. She inched closer to the mirror, looking for the reassurance that the moments before were in her head. As she neared the glass surface, her phone chimed. Resting on the screen was a notification from an unknown sender. She opened the message and was faced with a smiling emoji.

Daphne looked up from her phone and into the mirror once more. The woman was waiting for her. She smiled, then quickly laughed. As the laughing continued, cracks formed in the mirror's surface. The cracks grew, splintering the image of the woman. Daphne froze in place.

The glass continued to fracture, distorting the woman's image. Breaking free, the glass shards launched toward Daphne. She screamed as the fragments pierced her flesh. Shards embedded into her chest. Slivers slashed her throat. Her eyes were impaled by jagged glass. Blood streamed from her body. She could not scream. She could not see. She could not breath. Daphne was trapped. Blood spurted out of her mouth.

As blood poured out of her eye sockets and chest, she heard the woman laughing. She reached blindly for the doorknob. Turning the knob, the door opened. As she collapsed to the floor, she was met by the laughing of the woman and the mewing of a small cat.

22

Daphne's screams cut through the air. The group looked around at each other, noticing a member of their party was missing. Brian and Marcus rushed in the direction of her cry. Fumbling through the darkness, they arrived under the stairs. They could not have prepared themselves for what awaited them.

Even in the poorly, candlelit corridor they gained full measure of the display. Daphne lay on her side, blood pouring out of her eyes, neck, chest, and arms. Marcus used the light of his phone to gain a greater understanding of her injuries.

"Marcus?" Brian asked, waiting for some acknowledgment or recognition from his friend about what had happened to Daphne.

"This is pretty fucked up, man," Marcus replied as he rose.

Approaching footsteps alerted them. Brian positioned himself to meet whoever had followed them. Lois, Dolores, and Donna passed into the hallway before being obstructed by Brian.

"You don't want to go in there," he warned.

Knowing that Daphne was the only one missing from their quartet, the three feared the worst.

"What happened?" Donna asked.

"You don't need to see this," Marcus said as he tried to spare them the details of their friend's demise. Looking past the two, Donna could make out her friend's figure laying limp on the floor. The realization of her death was clear. Donna did not despair. She did not panic. Her focus turned from the safety and wellbeing of her friend to her own. The shock of the event permitted her to consider her own survival, her own life. Dolores and Lois, comforted by Brian, walked back to the dining area with the others. Donna stood in silence as she looked at her friend and images of being in her place flooded her thoughts.

Marcus grabbed her lightly by the shoulder coaxing her to return with the others. She brushed him off as she thought about how she would make it through the final hours. She took another look at her friend before departing.

Returning to the dining room, Brian and Marcus informed the others about Daphne's death. Calista shook her head as Brian and Marcus broke the news. Anne watched as the others returned to their previous spots in the room.

They passed several moments in silence. Calista continued to read before stopping at another entry in the book. She looked up, seeing several of the others asleep, she motioned to Lucinda who sat across from her at the table absorbed in her thoughts. Lucinda joined Calista as she held the book open to a particular passage and spread some of the letters on to the table.

"I think I understand what is happening in the house," she said confidently.

"How? What?" Lucinda responded in confusion.

"Look. She said if her blood were spilled on these grounds, she would return to terrorize those who violated her legacy?" she asked.

"Yeah, but how does that explain how we get out of here?" Lucinda asked.

"For generations, the family would not stay overnight on the grounds. Jayne pointed out that with the tours and anyone using the home, they could not stay past the agreed upon times. What if the reason why is because they knew it was cursed, but they were somehow honoring her wishes... something that she stated before her death to her children?" Calista added.

"That's quite a stretch," Lucinda replied.

"More of a stretch than all of the stuff that has taken place tonight? That's the only thing I could focus on... the why. Why would they allow people to visit, but not stay? Why would they open this home up a few decades ago? The family isn't hurting financially so opening it up to make money doesn't make sense," Calista continued.

Lucinda just stared blankly waiting for her to continue.

"I found the reason, or, at least, I think it's the reason why," she said as she unfolded two more letters, placing them on the table. "This is correspondence between her and Marie Laveau where she is asking for protection. This letter here is one in a series of threats made against her by a man named LeMonde."

"What does all this mean?" Lucinda asked.

"Looking at this, and the many entries that Victoria made, it's clear that she knew someone was going to try and kill her because of what she had done in organizing free blacks to vote and that they apparently knew she was using this house as a way to smuggle runaway slaves out of the south before the war," Calista added.

"So, what are you proposing?" Lucinda

inquired.

"We contact her," she stated with conviction.

"That... that is some white people shit," Lucinda replied. "It might be the only shot we have at getting out of here. I know you brother said wait until sunrise but is there any guarantee that any of us will make it until then?" she asked.

"Fuck it. What do we need to do?"

"Since there are only a few of us remaining, we are all going to need to participate," she offered.

Walking through the room, Calista and Lucinda informed the others about their plan. Met with some resistance, the two persuaded the group with the use of the letters and written entries in the book. They sat at the table, each placing a lit candle in front of them. Taking each other's hands, Calista called out instructions to them.

"Have you done this before?" Brian asked, looking at her.
"First time, but I've seen it done in the movies... can't be much different than that."

"You've got to be kidding me," Lois said under her breath.

"I am. The process is laid out in the book," she said, responding with an added wink. "Now, make sure that you remain holding each other's hands until we are done."

"How will we know when we are done?" Anne asked.

"We're about to find out," Calista replied.

Calista asked everyone to raise their hands over their heads and recite the words she stated. They reluctantly followed her instructions. She read from the book placed in front of her, asking for the spirit of Victoria Blanc to appear. Her request was met with silence. She repeated the words. The others followed. The storm continued raging outside as they repeated the words once more.

"Madame Blanc, if you are here, please give us a sign," Calista said in a firm tone.

The candles flickered and one by one, they extinguished. The flashes of lightning providing the only illumination in the room. The constant strikes permitted the group to see each other in the room.

"Everyone, remember, do not let go of each other," Calista instructed.

A low rumble emerged from the ceiling above the table. Their grips tightened. They looked upward. The fixtures swayed gently.

Calista looked to the table, focusing on the centerpiece. She again asked Victoria Blanc to give them a sign. The flames on the candles reignited. Caught off guard, Calista paused.

"What do we do now?" asked Brian.

"Oh yes. We should ask her something," she responded, regaining her bearings. "Madame Blanc, are you here with us?"

"*Yes,*" a whisper responded from overhead.

"What is it you want?" Calista asked.

"*My home,*" the voice answered.

"What do you mean, 'your home?'"

"*Why are you here in my home?*"

Confused, Calista paused before continuing her connection with Victoria.

"We... we are here visiting your home."

"*You don't belong here,*" she responded. "*You must leave.*"

"What do you mean?" Calista asked.

There was no response. The candles flickered bouncing light and shadows off the walls. The group looked around waiting for another sign or message from Victoria. The thunder rolled, adding to the anxiety of those at the table.

"Is it over? I mean... are we done with this?" Lois asked.

"I don't think so," Calista replied.

The hair on her arms raised. The flames of the candles leaned in her direction. Anne, seeing the movement of the light was dumbfounded. In disbelief, she moved her head closer to the flame and blew at the candle in front of her. It would not extinguish. The fire from the candles extended, drawing a more direct line toward

Calista. As Calista closed her eyes, the flames from the candles returned to their previous positions.

"*Why are you in my home?*" Calista asked, her eyes changing from dark brown to a rich hazel.

Lucinda's eyes widened as Calista's hand went cold in hers.

"Guys?" Lucinda asked.

"*Why are you here in my home?*" Calista questioned.

"What are you talking about, Calista?" Brian asked.

"*Why are you in my home?*" she repeated.

"This isn't funny," Donna stated.

"No, I am not playing this game with that weirdo. She has rubbed me the wrong way since we got on the bus. Now she is pretending to be possessed?" Lois said, rising from the table.

Brian and Dolores gripped her hands tighter preventing her from leaving.

"Let go, I'm not playing anymore. This isn't funny," Lois said, angrily.

"*This is not a game,*" Calista said from across the table. "*If you fail to honor my land, my home... you will never leave here alive.*"

"What do you want?" Lucinda asked shakily.

"*Truth,*" she replied.

"This is ridiculous!" Lois blurted, trying to stand.

Calista's eyes opened, focusing on Lois. She froze at her glare. Lois tried to open her mouth. Overcome with terror, she could not manage to separate her lips. Sitting in her chair, she did not move.

Lucinda, holding Calista's cold hand asked her a question which she did not want the answer.

"Who are you?"

"*Victoria Blanc*," the voice from Calista's body sternly answered.

"What do you want?" Lucinda continued.

"*You must leave this home with the truth,*" Victoria continued.

"What truth?" Brian interjected.

"*This home is a haven for the lost. Those who seek to take... those who seek to hurt... those who seek to bury or deny the truth will never leave these grounds,*" Victoria answered.

"What happened to you?" Lucinda asked.

"*I died here. Francis LeMonde and his men killed me right outside of my home. They wanted me to be afraid of them and their power. I did not yield or bend to their will,*" she continued. "*This is my land. This is my home. I never submitted to the will of any man after I married Charles.*"

"Your husband?" Anne asked.

"*Yes... but he was never my husband in spirit. I married him at the direction of my father. My family had passed as white since coming from San Domingue. When they arrived, customs thought our people were white, so they did not object or correct them. My family knew what being white in this country meant. With that power and freedom, there were no limits on what we could do. My father worked as a merchant making connections with people all throughout New Orleans. He heard about the plight of Negroes here and did what he could to help.*"

"How did he help?" Lucinda asked.

"*He had me marry Charles,*" Victoria answered.

"What do you mean," Brian followed.

"*Charles had wealth, privilege, and land. He saw me working in my father's office and thought that I would be in awe of his name and money. I was, but not for the reason he thought. I was young, beautiful, and as far as he knew, naive. We married in New Orleans, and I accompanied him to this home. I saw unspeakable things here. Nothing my father could say about what happened at plantations could prepare me for the true monsters of this land.*"

"What do you mean? What happened?" Brian asked.

"*Charles happened,*" Victoria replied.

The group was dumbstruck at her answer. They didn't know what to make of the response. Aware of their confusion, Victoria elaborated.

"*I walked in on Charles ripping the teeth out of one of the men, a slave named Curtis. He caught Curtis taking food from the pantry. Charles had him chained up, beaten, burned with a torch, and then began prying the teeth from his mouth. I didn't know what to do, but my father's words stayed with me as to why I was put in this place.*"

"Which were?" Marcus asked.

"*My father told me that I would be their salvation. I could help them escape this horrid institution. He told me of all the slave revolts that had taken place in this land and that it always led to something worse. My father made sure that I exercised caution and played the role necessary for the men and women on this plantation to become free. When I found Charles torturing that man, a rage grew in me. It was an anger I had never felt. I grabbed Charles, trying to pull him off of Curtis. Charles pushed me to the ground. The fire built inside of me even more. I saw that poor soul was bleeding everywhere. His weeping and breathing were the only sign that he was alive, as faint as it was.*" Victoria took a deep breath before continuing.

"What happened?"

"There was a knife on the ground. Charles had been using it to carve flesh from that man. I drove the blade into his back. Charles screamed in pain. He tried in vain to pull the knife out. I grabbed the key from his waist, releasing Curtis from the shackles. Scared, Curtis froze, the only thing holding him in place was the shock and disbelief at what I did. Writhing on the ground, Charles cursed my name and pleaded for Curtis to kill me. The screams were heard by other slaves in the house who made their way to the cellar. Charles called to the men and women standing at the door saying, 'If you niggers know what is good for you, you'll get down here and help me.'

"They didn't move. Curtis stood over Charles and helped him to his feet. I was shocked to see this man help Charles after what had happened to him until he started walking with him. Charles told Curtis to pull the knife out to which Curtis said, 'nah, massa, I can't.' Charles cursed the man to no end. Curtis called one of the other men down. Each took one of Charles' arms in their hands. Holding him up, they forced him against the wall. The men bound his wrists in the shackles. Curtis asked for me to depart from the cellar saying that a decent woman like me shouldn't see what they were going to do. I refused, watching as the men took turns pulling Charles' teeth out with the pliers he dropped on the ground."

Horrified and shocked at the words of Victoria, several around the table sat wide-eyed and jaws agape.

"We left him in the cellar where he wasted away until his death," she continued. "When he died, we took him out and buried him at the far end of the property. After the things I saw him do and the things the slaves told me that he did to them, I didn't want them to have to deal with Charles being anywhere in their proximity, even in death."

"But Victoria, why did you continue to own slaves?" Anne asked.

"I owned no one," she responded, firmly. "I inherited all of Charles' land and holdings of which there were over a hundred slaves. I assembled the men, women, and children and had them tell me their stories. Every single one of them spoke of pain. There was nothing joyful about their lives or their experiences here. When I asked them about leaving, it was clear there were no safe options. For those who desired, I arranged freedom papers for them. Unfortunately, the first few men and women freed were met with violence by white mobs outside of New Orleans. When they returned, we knew there was only *one option: project a facade. I continued in my role as slave mistress and they as my enslaved. I adopted their children, sending them to Negro schools and universities after the war."*

Victoria continued explaining to the group how she presented the image of a wealthy slaveholder in the years preceding the Civil War noting that she only traveled to New Orleans to visit with her father or to conduct business. Anne, Lucinda, Brian, and Marcus continued asking questions of Victoria. Dolores and Donna did not know what to make of the events they witnessed. Lois, in disbelief, struggled to process the interactions taking place between those seated at the table.

Nervously, Lucinda looked into Victoria's eyes, unsure about the question she needed to ask as it came out of her lips.

"Victoria, why are you killing us?" Lucinda asked, shakily.

"*That is the price of dark magic. That is the cost of my blood being shed on these grounds,*" she responded.

"I don't understand," Lucinda stated.

"*My spirit has remained in this house, undisturbed for many years. When I asked Madame Laveau for help before I died, she warned me of the consequences,*" Victoria continued.

"Which are?" Brian asked.

"The rage, the fire, the anger that lived in me remained. The horrors that I witnessed and were recounted to me, released something in my spirit, in my soul. It is something that could not be controlled, not even by me," Victoria stated, firmly.

"How... how can me make it out of here?" Marcus asked.

"The rage lives as long as the truth is hidden," she said. Releasing Lucinda and Anne's hands, pointed to the book Calista placed on the table after finding it in the flooring. *"This holds the truth."*

Glimmers of light entered the room. A reddish–orange haze bounced off the walls. The sun broke through the clouds as the rain had ceased while the group sat at the table. Lois looked at her watch.

It was just a few minutes after six AM.

Her patience exhausted in the early hours of the morning while Victoria regaled them with her history. She grew bored and unconvinced of the stories that had come out of Calista's mouth.

As the sunlight increased the illumination of the room, the hazel in Calista's eyes dwindled. Marcus, noticing this change called out to Victoria. Lucinda, aware of Marcus' action felt the warmth return to Calista's hand.

"Calista?" she asked, lowering her head to

meet her eyes.

"Yes?" she replied, confused.

"Is that you?"

Disoriented, Calista questioned her state, looking around the room.

"Why is it so bright in here?" she asked.

"You don't remember anything that happened?" Lucinda asked her.

"What are you talking about? We were questioning Victoria and then it was all blurry and bright in here," Calista responded.

The group broke their hold on one another. Brian rose and stood over his sister and Calista. Placing his hand on her shoulder, he informed her of what took place. The news, although jarring, comforted her in knowing that there was more history of this home and this woman to be explored. Standing from the table, she looked around the room, seeing it with new eyes and a renewed determination to search for the truth.

23

Sitting in silence, the group questioned Victoria's message. They questioned whether they would be able to leave the home safely. They were certain in her words that there was still a risk to their lives despite her telling them the truth of her history. None of them wanted to risk tempting their fate or further test Victoria's patience or offend her.

Lucinda looked up from the table, placing her hand on her brother's arm. Whispering in his ear, she rose and walked out of the room. He followed her into the library.

"What is it?" Brian asked.

"I really need to show you something," she said, walking to the bookshelf before pulling at the release she found earlier.

A click sounded from behind the shelf as it inched away from the wall. Lucinda opened the shelf wide and propped the entrance open with one of the chairs in the room. She looked to her brother, imploring him to follow her. Lighting one of the lanterns, she descended the stairs leading into the cellar. Brian walked behind her, confused.

"Brian, I tried to tell you about this earlier, but I didn't know how to explain it. I found myself down here earlier. There was something... someone down here," she said with her eyes fixed on the cellar walls.

"What was it?" he asked.

"I'm not sure. I actually thought it was a person down here," she said before stopping as she returned to where she first found the figure in the cellar. "Here. It was here. See this," she said pointing to a few small, white objects on the ground.

"I heard its voice coming from the wall... I briefly saw its face. After what Victoria told us, it made more sense."

Brian looked in the direction of the lantern's light. Teeth were scattered on the ground. Next to them were shackles and broken chains. Brian grabbed a link, inspecting it.

"Find anything?" Calista called from the top of the stairs. Marcus and the others followed her into the room.

"Yeah. You need to see this," Brian responded.

Calista, carefully descended into the cellar. Walking up to Brian, she was overcome with anxious energy.

"What is it?" she asked.

"Looks like the next step in your research," Brian replied handing her the chains

She pored over the chains before grabbing one of the shackles from the ground. Despite the oxidation and conditions of the cellar, the metal was in good condition. Calista brushed her thumb over the mechanism, uncovering the foundry which made the restraints. Overcome with excitement over the discovery, Calista's knees buckled, and she dropped the shackles and links to the ground. Brian and Lucinda caught her before she fell, as well. As they helped her to her feet, Calista patted them on the back. A large grin formed on her face.

"This is our key out of here," she said.

"What do you mean?" Brian asked.

"Victoria said we need to honor this home and its history and that we need to pass on the truth of what happened here. This must be what she was talking about. This place isn't just cursed because of what happened to her, it's cursed because of what happened here and that it has gone ignored. This, the book, the documents, these things will allow the full story of this place to be told. Not only does this reframe the narrative of this house and its history, but it also exposes the men that murdered Victoria," Lucinda informed him.

Calista picked up one of the shackles, exiting the cellar. She passed the others who were waiting in the library. She ran her fingers over the iron, soaking in the history, absorbing the pain before kneeling on the floor. She knew the meaning of that shackle more than anyone else in the room. This was not just something that was used to control and bind the enslaved, but this was something that symbolized fear, the fear that white southerners had of these men and women. It was something that they used to demonstrate their power over another human being.

Lucinda watched Calista as she caressed the artifact. She grew concerned as she thought about the words that came out of her mouth from Victoria. The cellar is where she found her husband torturing the enslaved. Her father had arranged for her marriage to Charles knowing that the money and power could possibly change her, but he also understood that his daughter had the ability to unravel the system and would not be enchanted or corrupted by its enticements.

The sun grew brighter. The fixtures and decorations throughout the room came back to life, their beauty hidden in the darkness that the night brought.

The group walked toward the front entrance, the death and terror still fresh in their minds. Those who gained a bit of comfort in the rising sun were reminded of the horrors that took place in the home as they passed Margaret's mangled body. They moved solemnly as they gathered at the front door.

Grabbing the knob, Brian closed his eyes anticipating something horrific to befall him. As he turned the knob, the door cracked open. He pulled the door, opening it wide. The smell of the wet earth penetrated the entrance. The relaxing, familiar sent relaxed the group as they stepped on to the porch. They each looked around for something that would signify the guarantee of their safety. Seeing Eli's body on the ground did not reassure them that danger had become a stranger to the grounds. They cautiously stepped down from the porch on to the soft mud at the base of the home. The water had receded, allowing the mud to only reach the base of their shoes.

Marcus jogged over to the bus, the squishing of the ground meeting each of his steps. He stumbled suddenly, his foot snagging on something sticking out from the ground. As he regained his balance, he took note of the small root just above the surface alerting the others. Arriving at the bus, he looked through the glass door. He held on to hope that there were spare keys inside allowing them to leave. Walking around the bus, he checked each of the windows yearning for one to be unlocked or slightly ajar. As he rounded the right side of the bus, he noticed a window near the back of the vehicle provided him with relief as he could see the manual lock was unlatched.

Marcus placed his foot on the back wheel, lifting himself to a better position. Placing his hands flat on the glass, he slid the window down. He reached inside of the opening, grabbing at the metal sides. He pulled himself up, quickly realizing that he was not slender enough to fit through.

"Lucy!" he called over. "I need your help."

She quickly joined him at the tire. After his assistance in mounting the tire, she slid through the window. From the inside, she unlatched the door, securing entrance for the others. She stepped down from the bus, meeting Marcus outside. Looking past him, she could see that the others had stopped a short distance away from the bus with Brian squatting next to the root Marcus had tripped over.

Marcus and Lucinda walked over to them hoping to understand the cause of their delay. As they reached them, there was confusion and a solemn demeanor with most of the group. Anne stared at the ground, the roots they assumed had been unearthed by the storm were too familiar to her. The emerald ring was unmistakable. Her friend Trudy had received it when she graduated from college. She went everywhere with it. As Lucinda looked closer, she could see the burgundy nail polish. Trudy was another victim of this land.

"There's nothing we can do for her now," Brian said, trying to comfort the group. "We need to see if we can get the bus started."

Anne nodded before kneeling and touching her friend's hand. The group walked back to the bus together. As they entered, the weight of the night forced some to collapse into their seats. Calista, holding the chains and Victoria's book sat silently. Marcus scoured the glove box hoping to find a spare set of keys. All he could find were old maps, parking tickets, and matchbooks.

"Looks like we're out of luck. Does anyone have a signal so we can try the police or someone?"

No one responded. Marcus checked his phone, seeing only his reflection in the dead screen. He sat down in the driver's seat contemplating what steps were available. Reaching under the seat, he found a small tool kit. Opening it, he discovered a large flathead screwdriver. Considering his limited options Marcus drove the blade of the screwdriver into the ignition. It would not turn. Frustrated, he tossed the screwdriver behind him into the aisle.

Although disappointed, everyone continued resting and patiently waiting in the hopes that someone would arrive on the property. With the rain ending and the water receding, they anticipated the arrival of the police from their call the previous night. No vehicles approached on the horizon. There was no salvation for them. The waiting on the inside of the house filled them with anxiety and fear. The waiting on the outside left them empty.

With the door open, Marcus could hear dragging noises outside of the bus. Hearing the soft crunching sound, Marcus raised his head off the steering wheel. He focused his attention outside, hoping to hear the noise again. Looking in the mirrors, he could see nothing. The windows and mirrors fogged over.

Sitting in the driver's seat, Marcus faced the others and placed his finger over his mouth, signaling them to stay quiet. Marcus strained to look through the foggy glass and determine what was outside. His concentration was broken as a something impacted the side of the bus. Startled, everyone sat up in their seats.

They could not see what lurked outside. They waited for it to emerge. Marcus pulled the handle, closing the door, placing a barrier between what was outside and those on the bus. Another object impacted the wall of the bus. Marcus attempted to find the source by looking at the side mirrors, but there was nothing there he could find.

Another slam. Several of the group held their breath. The tension was broken as a hand holding a set of keys slammed against the window of the door. Recognizing the face behind the raised hand, Marcus smiled. He opened the door ushering Robert in. Shocked at his reappearance, the group barraged him with questions.

Robert, breathing heavily, raised his hands calming the riders.

"I'm sorry y'all. I was out on the road and got attacked by a snake. I'm embarrassed to say that I passed out from shock. When I came to, I tried walking back to the house, but the way was blocked from the rain washing out the road. I couldn't safely get back and had to stay in one of the old slave cabins. I would have called, but I left my phone on the bus. Where is everyone?" he asked.

"Dead," Calista coldly responded.

"What do you mean, dead?" he asked.

The group, frenzied, listed off the names of their friends who perished during the night. Robert recoiled at hearing the news about Jayne, Daphne, Eric, Trudy, Eli, and Margaret.

"What do y'all wanna do?" he asked, struggling to stay upright after hearing them recount what happened.

"What do you mean?" Brian responded.

"I mean, do y'all want me to call the police on the radio and wait or do you want to go to them?" he returned.

The group sat, considering their options. Lois rose, angrily.

"I want to get the fuck out of here!" she yelled, stomping her foot for extra emphasis.

"We need to wait," Brian responded. "If Robert can call the police from his radio on the bus, we shouldn't just leave. What about all the people in that house? Should we just leave them in the hopes that we'll make it to the station and have the police come out here?"

"I don't give a shit! We need to go!" she added.

"What about Daphne, are we just going to leave her here?" Donna asked.

"Fuck her! She shouldn't have walked off. If she stayed with us, she would still be alive! I'm not staying here and dying to make any of you comfortable or because you feel guilty!" she continued.

Lois stormed to the front of the bus, walking up to Robert. Despite the height disparity between the two, Lois wagged her finger, barking orders at him. She threatened legal action against him if he did not start the engine.

"Is this who you want to really spend your life with?" Lucinda asked.

Lois' actions sunk in for Brian. She looked so small to him. Everything real about her became apparent. Everything Marcus and his sister had warned him about came into better focus.

"Lois," he said placing his hand on her shoulder.

"What the fuck do you want?" she screamed, pushing him away from her.

"You need to calm down. I think we need to—"

"I don't give a fuck what you think. In fact, I don't give a fuck about what any of you think! Fuck this house! Fuck that bitch, Victoria! We made it out, why do we need to dwell on them?" Lois yelled, pointing her finger at all of the other riders. She turned to Robert "Now drive!"

Brian watched as she berated her friends for wanting to stay. Walking to her again, anger rose in him.

"Lois!" he yelled.

"What?" she shot back.

"When we get back, we're done."

"What do you mean, done?"

"Done."

"Oh. I should have known. It's fine by me." She said, taking off her engagement ring, handing it to Brian. He sat down, putting the ring in his pocket.

The rumble of the engine caught Lois' attention. She turned, approaching Robert. As he put the bus in gear, the transmission forced the vehicle to jump forward. Caught off guard, Lois lost her balance, falling forward. As she reached out to one of the seats, she stumbled, failing to grasp one of the handles. Lois tumbled to the floor, impacting the worn carpet in the aisle.

"You alright back there?" Robert asked.

Lois did not respond. Marcus looked down at her.

"Jesus Christ, she's dramatic," he scoffed. "Brian finally stands up to her and she throws a fit."

Lois lay prone on the floor.

"Come on, get up," Donna called to her friend.

She lay still.

Brian walked over to help her from the ground. Grabbing her shoulder, he felt something sticky on the floor. Pulling his hand back, his fingertips were covered red. He cautiously grabbed

Lois by the shoulder, patting her. As she did not respond, he turned her over and was greeted by an unwelcome sight.

Lois' hair covered her face. As Brian brushed her hair away, he found the black and yellow handle of a screwdriver embedded in her left eye socket, the shank piercing her brain. Shocked, her friends screamed. Lucinda looked on in bewilderment, her hands covering her mouth. Marcus sat in silence as he tried processing the quick turn in events. Stupefied, Brian sat himself in the nearest seat.

Robert, after checking Lois' vital signs placed a jacket he kept behind his seat over her torso, covering her face. Before returning to the wheel, he looked and nodded at everyone assuring them that he would get them safely to the authorities. He put the bus in gear and drove the vehicle down the road. The wheels sloshed through the muddy puddles that filled once gravel path.

Robert didn't know how to properly console his passengers given the news that they informed him of and the incident that had taken place on the bus. He tried to carry on conversations with them, but his mind carefully evaluated what would be appropriate at the given time.

Usually a man with the gift of gab and a strong conversationalist, he had nothing more he could say other than announcing the streets they approached on their way back to New Orleans or stating how much time remained before they would arrive at the nearest station.

After a drive that was only plagued with drying roads and the occasional driver who failed to use their turn signal, the group arrived outside of a small Sheriff station in the outskirts of New Orleans. The passengers descended the steps solemnly. Robert thanked them and offered his condolences and apologies to each as they disembarked.

Calista sat quietly on the bus as the others exited. Still holding on to Victoria's leather-bound book and the chain found in the cellar, she looked up to Robert who was standing in the aisle.

"Ma'am, we're here," he assured her.

"Oh. Thank you," she said, rising.

Robert guided her to the door apologizing again. Calista turned, thanking him for getting them to the station safely.

"You are welcome, ma'am," he offered.

"You have been a great help," she responded, looking up at him with her bright, hazel eyes.

About the Author

Donald R. Guillory is an author, historian, educator, and cohost of the podcast, TheNecronomi.com. Donald is also the author of *The Token Black Guide: Navigations Through Race in America* and *Bastards of the Bayou*.

Follow the author on Twitter @donguillory

www.DonaldRGuillory.com